RAILING THE RAILING

A SENTIENT OBJECT ROMANCE

OBJECTS OF DESIRE

ANNARA LAYNE

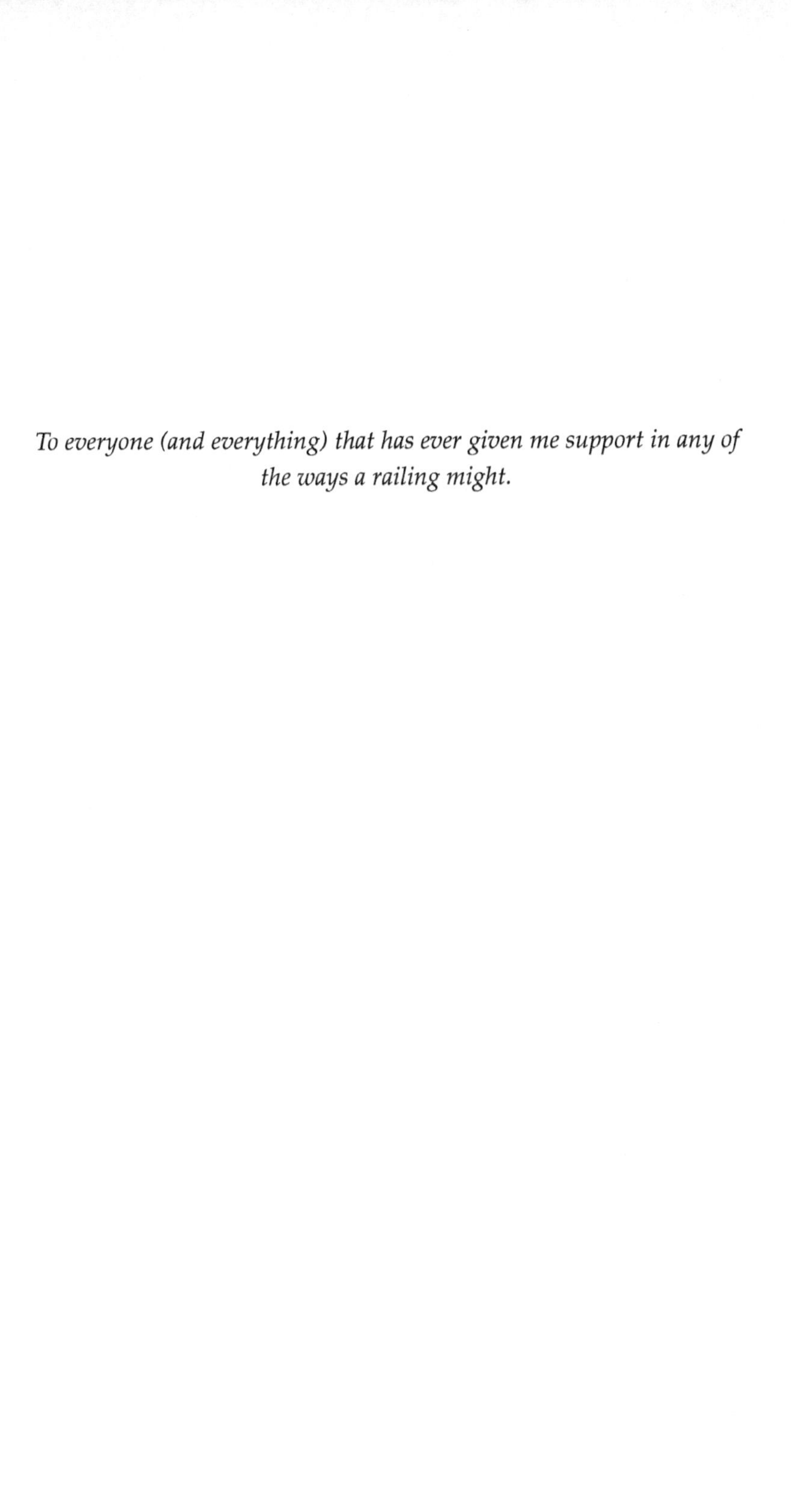

To everyone (and everything) that has ever given me support in any of the ways a railing might.

A NOTE FOR READERS

This book is a little different from the first two, in that there are two love interests: the railing, and a human man. I know some readers gravitate to sentient object for reasons that might make Luca's presence unwelcome. If that's the case for you, I fully understand you setting this book aside.

CHAPTER ONE

I STARE AT THE PHONE, silently begging it to ring. It's a corded phone, and the black coils twist over themselves, because somehow, I never got around to updating the front desk phone to something manufactured after the 1990s.

There was a time I would have smoothed out the kinks in the phone cord, wanting everything to be perfect, but there's no point now; it's not like there's anyone around to see it.

The upside is I have a lot of time on my hands.

Like, master virtual chess despite never having played before last year, kind of time.

I sigh and slump across the counter. We were at half capacity over the holidays, and I thought that momentum would continue into the new year so we could finally get the books back in the black. But no; it turns out all the guests we had only stayed at the inn because all the other options were full.

And honestly, I don't blame them. People deserve the best, and Sunnyside Inn hasn't been the best in a few years.

Tears fill my eyes when I think about all the hard work my Aunt Britney put into this place over the years. When she bought it, it was an old, dilapidated house that was seconds away from being condemned. She spent years fixing it up, pouring all of her time and money into it. Everyone told her it was a fool's errand, that *nobody* would ever be able to turn this place into a sought-after destination, and *especially* not a girl with no business degree and only one year of customer service under her belt. But, as she so often does, Aunt Britney proved them wrong. Within a year of opening, the inn was on lists of best accommodations in the state, and people came from all over the world specifically to stay here.

When people asked who ran the inn, people would honest to god answer "It's Britney, bitch."

Nobody's said that about me since I took over.

For reasons beyond the fact that my name's Wren, not Britney.

I grew up spending most of my time at the inn, the child of the manager and the head chef. Aunt Britney didn't hire family unless they were the best, and my parents, indisputably, were the best. They still are, though "the best" looks different in retirement. My mom, Brit's sister, now focuses on planning trips for the three of them, and she's truly incredible at finding deals. They travel 100% of the time, and their monthly expenses are about what some families spend on a long weekend at a certain magical theme park.

My father went from running a kitchen to studying in as many as possible: he takes classes with local chefs (both professional ones and random home cooks they meet on their travels) so he can learn all the different types of cuisines. He was always good, but now every meal he makes it truly out of this world.

Brit's just kind of along for the ride. After decades of running a successful inn, she'd finally enjoying getting to be the guest instead of the person behind the desk.

The inn was a dream job for all three of them, and it set them up to have the kind of retirement most people can only dream of.

I've known I wanted to follow in Brit's and my parents' footsteps pretty much my whole life. I didn't just want to work here when I grew up; I wanted to run it when they all retired. I didn't want someone else swooping in and claiming seniority over me in my own home. From the time I was in diapers, I learned everything I could from Aunt Brit and my parents, and when I graduated high school I went on to business school—even though Aunt Brit couldn't have cared less about the degree; she was proof that drive, experience, and savvy matter more than a four-year accredited program (with a Master's to boot, thank you very much).

And my work paid off; when she retired early to go travel the world like she'd always dreamed of, Aunt Brit left the inn to me. Two years later, my parents joined her. They'd seen me in action, and they all agreed that officially putting me in charge was a sound move. So, at the end of my parents' retirement party, Aunt Brit handed me the keys, both literally and figuratively: she placed the first set of keys she'd ever had made in my hand and wished me luck, "not that you'll need it."

Turns out that was the worst possible decision she could have made.

Not everything that's gone wrong has been my fault. In fact, most of the issues have been completely out of my control, like the HVAC system breaking in the middle of a blizzard, or the wasps that nested in the walls—and revealed themselves in all their angry, buzzy glory to a guest who was allergic.

Insurance covered her hospital bills, but insurance doesn't cover bad word-of-mouth. And frankly, I don't think her reaction was bad enough; if an inn almost killed me, I'd have left a *much* worse review.

But still, it's hard to look at these past few years and not feel bad about everything that's gone wrong, even if there was nothing I could have done to prevent most of it. If Aunt Brit were still in charge, the hornets would have taken one look at her and known she's a woman who's not to be trifled with. And I'm sure she would have found a way to coax the dead HVAC back to life, at least until the tech was able to get through all the snow.

Every time she calls to check in, I lie and say everything's going fine.

Well. Last time I didn't technically *lie*. It's not my fault she assumed I *wasn't* talking about a virtual chess match when I said things were going well.

If she'd explicitly asked about the inn, I would have given a very different answer.

For example, I might have told her (metaphorically; I wouldn't have *actually* told her) that I took a bunch of extra pictures of guests over Christmas so I can show her proof that we have paying customers even when we don't, actually.

I hate the lie, even if it's only implied, but I'd hate the look on her face when I let her down even more.

The truth is, for almost a year now, we've been making a quarter of the income we need to stay afloat. I'm talking *deeply* in the red.

Aunt Brit managed to operate the inn with better margins than most, so we had enough of a cushion that I wasn't initially worried when things started going wrong a few years ago. But now, it's gotten impossible to ignore.

If I don't figure something out soon, the inn that I've called home my entire life won't exist for much longer.

The phone rings, startling me enough that I let out a little shriek. I put my hand over my wildly beating heart with a laugh and take a few seconds to calm down, then look down at the receiver that's practically already in my hands.

"Hello? Sunnyside Inn, this is Wren speaking, how may I help you today?"

"Wren, it's Luca. I've got a solution to the banister problem."

Luca is my best friend Lucy's twin brother. Yes, their parents gave them basically the same name just one letter apart. At least when you say it out loud, their names sound pretty different. On paper is where it gets tricky—Lucy found out Luca got into college before he did, because she misread the name on the envelope. And Luca has opened three separate medical letters of Lucy's—and learned some things about his sister that I'm sure will haunt him forever.

When we were kids, Lucy was over here so much some of the regulars thought she lived here, too, running through the halls of the inn and making up backstories for the guests. Luca mostly kept to himself, but he came over almost as often as Lucy did. Occasionally, we'd manage to convince him to hang out with us, but when we couldn't, he'd sit in the pergola or one of his increasingly obscure hiding spots and read, or write in one of the many notebooks he always carried with him. "I like it here," he'd say with a shrug when we'd open a cabinet to find him curled in the dark with a flashlight pointed at his little notebook.

He might not quite be family, not even in the slightly-removed way Lucy is, but he gets why this place is so special.

"The banister problem," as we've taken to calling it, is a crack in the railing of our main staircase, which I noticed a couple weeks ago. It's small enough that if we actually had guests, they probably wouldn't even notice it, but it's been slowly worsening, and I have serious concerns about its structural integrity. Especially with the luck we've been having the past few years, if it's not a safety concern now it will be soon, and yet another person getting injured on the property is the last thing I need to add to the growing list of concerns.

"Please tell me it's cheap," I beg. Luca is the only person who knows the extent of the inn's financial troubles, and that's only because he walked in one day to find me crying over the books. He wanted me to tell my family, or at least Lucy, but I refused. I don't want them to know how much of a failure I am.

"Even better. It's free."

"Thank fucking god," I mutter.

"No, not god; thank fucking *me*," he teases.

My mind trips over the words "fucking me" coming from Luca. I would love to. But he's off limits.

For *so* many reasons.

"I'll wait and see how good this solution is before I even considering putting *you* and *fucking* in the same sentence, thank you very much."

"You wound me, Wren." He acts affronted, but I can hear his smile through the phone.

"Keep it in your pants, Luca. Someday. *If* you earn it."

It's a running joke between us, that we'll eventually have sex. It started one night in college when Lucy got drunk and took us both by the hand with a very serious expression on her face. "This is very, very, very, *very* important, okay?" she slurred. Honestly, I may have even forgotten some of the *verys*. Luca and I looked at each other, worried. She'd been kind of withdrawn in the weeks leading up to it, refusing to tell either of us what was wrong, which was unlike her, and we were both concerned. The look that passed between us conveyed that we were both committed to helping her with whatever she was about to confess. Drugs or shitty boys or money problems—whatever it was, we were there.

"I love you both so much," she said, tears filling her eyes. "You're my two best friends in the whole entire freakin' world." When Lucy gets drunk, she speaks like a child. It's adorable as hell. "I need you to know that if you ever get married that's okay with me. More than okay, actually. But only if I can be the maid of honor *and* the best man. Or the person who makes you say 'I do.' The priest person. I could get ordained. I like religions, I really could do it." She said it so earnestly that it genuinely made me wonder if someone had told her she couldn't.

"Babe, I don't think we're gonna get married," I told her gently. "You don't have to worry about that."

"That's why I'm worried," she wailed. And by wailed, I mean she was crying actual, literal tears. Not that I can judge; I've gotten way weirder when drunk. "I'm scared you won't ever get married and it will be all because of me, because you're scared of hurting my feelings, when actually you'll hurt my feelings if you *don't* get married."

"Lucy," Luca said, putting his arm around her shoulder, "let's talk about this in the morning, okay?"

She sniffled. "Okay."

We put her to bed, laughing at the absurdity of Lucy trying to push us together. When we brought it up in the morning, she had no memory of the conversation.

I figured out later, through the grapevine, that one of the girls in her class tried to antagonize her by lying and saying that Luca and I were sneaking around behind her back. And, like the absolute gem she is, rather than getting mad at us, Lucy worked hard to be okay with it, which was sweet but misguided, considering nothing has ever happened between us—and nothing ever will.

We joke about it to this day, though.

And if I'm honest with myself, I really wouldn't *mind* something happening with Luca.

He's sweet and charming, the kind of guy I would trust to hold my drink at a party and walk me home when I'm blackout drunk. He still carries around a notebook with him, just like he did as a kid. There's a new one almost every week, but he won't let anyone see inside. I caught a glimpse of it once and it was the most beautiful poetry about the boughs over the pergola he spent his childhood in.

My pergola.

On top of all that, he's also a handyman, and has the muscles to show for it. Basically, he's the whole package, and after that night with Lucy (and my already years-long crush on him at that point), I realized I had two options: lean into the joke of us being together or get too awkward to be around him at all.

It's fine. I'm a grown woman. I can handle joking about the things I think of when I'm alone in my bed at night. I definitely don't have to force my tho0ughts away from the beginnings of a naughty little fantasy so I can focus on his real-world solution to my very real problem.

"Oh, the solution is *definitely* good enough to warrant thank-*fucking*-me."

CHAPTER TWO

THE RAILING IS FUCKING GORGEOUS. It's made of a wood that Luca could probably name but all I know is it's dark, free of knots, and polished so to the point it gleams.

Honestly?

Between the richness in the color and the shine, there's something almost sensual about this railing.

Very sensual.

Or maybe I just need to get laid.

I *definitely* need to get laid, if I'm having these thoughts about a literal piece of wood.

The whole railing is one continuous piece, unlike our current one, which, if you look closely enough, you'll see is made of two straight pieces and a separate curling swoop down at the bottom all expertly joined together.

"Did you make this?" I breathe.

Luca shakes his head. "I found it in the back of the old shed, with a note on it saying it was for the main staircase." The old shed used to be where we kept all the special things, but after a pipe burst in one of the rooms, we shoved a bunch of stuff in there to keep it out of the way. That was almost eight years ago, a few years before Brit handed me the reigns; she must have bought this railing a long time ago, then forgotten about it in all the chaos of the flood.

"I called Britney and cleared it with her already," Luca continues. "I told her I was going through the shed to surprise you and thought it would be nice to replace the railing but didn't want you to stress about it. She thinks I'm doing it in secret."

"Why did you ask her? It's my inn." I try to tamp down my annoyance, but people have underestimated me my entire life and gone over my head for decisions that are actually mine to make. Luca's one of the few people who doesn't do that, and it stings that he would now.

"It's her piece of wood, technically. The receipt with it shows that she paid in cash, and you know she wasn't writing things off in the early days. She bought it right around the time the inn first opened. I assumed it would be okay, but I didn't want to risk replacing it and then having her call the next day saying she wants it, since it technically belongs to *her*, not the inn."

Okay, that makes sense. The fact that Luca is being so thorough and careful definitely doesn't warm my heart. Or other parts of me. Nope.

"Wait, why were you in the shed in the first place? Especially so deep into it?"

"Come here." He takes my hand just like he's done a million times. It doesn't mean anything, but it sends butterflies fluttering in my stomach anyway. I shove them aside. Considering Lucy had to get bonkers drunk to give us her blessing, this is a line I have no intention of ever actually crossing, no matter how much I might want to.

Okay, how much I *definitely* want to.

Luca leads me through the empty hall of the inn, through the kitchen that doesn't have any staff anymore because I can't afford to pay them to stand around and do nothing all day, and out into the back gardens. These, at least, look beautiful—I have enough free time to weed and plant and deadhead and everything else a garden needs, and Aunt Brit had a robust sprinkler system set up.

Luca and I wind between the brown bushes and bunches of ornamental kale, the one spot of color this time of year.

My breath clouds in front of me and I'm tempted to run back

inside for my jacket, but Luca is so excited I decide to just tough it out for a few minutes. It takes more than a few minutes to develop hypothermia.

I think.

"Voila!" Luca throws open the door of the shed.

And holy shit.

The last time I was out here I couldn't fully open the door because something in the pile of junk behind it had fallen and blocked it. Now, the door flies open, hitting the wall behind it with a bang, and revealing a clean, empty room. He's washed the windows, and sunlight streams through it, leaving the space light and airy.

"It's gorgeous," I breathe.

As kids, Lucy and I would pretend we lived in the shed, avoiding the small pile in the corner and playing house in the rest of the space. Sometimes we'd convince Luca to join us, and he and I would be the parents with Lucy as our child. We thought it was gross back then, pretending to be in love, but it was less gross than the twins doing it, so we dutifully went along with it.

Occasionally, we'd convince Luca to be the child and Lucy and I would be the parents, but he was always argued, citing that he didn't want to pretend to be a kid, seeing as he already was one in real life.

As if the other two of us weren't. But it never really bothered us the way it bothered him.

Now, looking at the outbuilding where we used to play house, I see all that potential again. It's large for a shed, big enough to be a perfect standalone studio apartment—and a spacious one, at that. There'd be space for a large bed, a couch, a coffee table—even a large wardrobe. There's already a sink for washing off tools, which would be easy to turn into a kitchenette.

"Luca." My voice comes out strangled, and he gives a pleased little hum beside me.

"You like it?"

"You did all this for me?"

"Yes and no."

I turn to him. "Okay, what does that mean?"

"I had a thought. There's work that needs to be done around the inn. I was thinking I could be your handyman, officially."

"And live here?" It's a good idea, but a part of me aches to be the one to take this space. It's selfish of me, especially after he spent what must have been dozens of hours cleaning it out.

"Here, or in your room, if you want to live here. But if I lived on the property and didn't have to pay rent, that would free up more of my time to help you out. I think we could turn things around together."

"You do? Really? Don't bullshit me, Luca."

"I'm not. I have a plan."

He sits on the floor of the shed and pulls a notebook out of his pocket, which he shoves my way so I can read through his plans. I flip through page after page of numbers, sketches, and hastily scribbled ideas.

My jaw literally drops.

His plans for the inn are brilliant, subtle changes that will make a world of difference, and I tell him how impressed I am.

"The shed is yours," I declare, setting the notebook down between us. "If you want it. If you'd rather have the room, you can have that instead. You deserve whichever space you want."

"Which do you want?" he asks, looking up at me intensely through his thick lashes. I swear my heart skips a beat.

I look away.

"Nope." I shake my head. "You did all this work. Take the one you want."

"It'll be a while until the shed is ready. My lease is up in a few weeks, so I'll work to make this space livable, and we can talk about it then, okay?"

I nod.

"Now, let's get started on some of this work."

I follow him inside and watch as he pries the current railing off the posts and sets it aside. "We can use that for something else. Maybe I can make little trinkets the guests can buy, so they can take a piece of the original inn home with them. I bet you could charge an absurd amount to the right person."

My chest aches at the thought of giving up a piece of my home to strangers, never to be seen again, but Luca has a point. A few years ago, something like that would go for $50 easily, even if it was just a piece of the wood stuck onto a keychain— even higher if it were carved into something special. Luca's right —if we can get customers back through the doors and show them that this place is still worth something, selling off pieces of the old railing could provide a good source of income. Especially since they'd be limited edition.

While Luca works on the railing, I fiddle with my social media plan. Aunt Brit never did much with social media, because she opened the inn before it the internet was really a thing, let along things like TikTok and Instagram, and by the time they got big she had enough word-of-mouth and magazine write-ups that she didn't need to waste time or money on advertising. By that point, the inn was booked out years in advance, so social media only would have added to our stress without adding anything meaningful; it's not like we could have taken on additional guests.

But many of the loyal clients are now old enough that they don't make the trip anymore, and their children are mostly going to more exciting places, like resorts in the Caribbean, cheaper places closer to home, or places that are more geared toward their own young children. In this economy, and in the age of the internet, it's hard to convince people to base their entire vacation around a beautiful inn whose whole shtick is quiet relaxation— and without the fancy spa experience that most people look for now in a place like this.

We don't actually have social media for the inn yet; I want to have a solid strategy in place before I make any of the accounts, because there's nothing worse than an account with only a few paltry posts, or posts that don't adhere to a specific, clear brand.

I finalize my plans for the Instagram page and make a mock feed of the first few posts. I plan to start with three posts on day one, then post daily for a week, and then move to 3-4 times a week. I don't want too many posts with zero engagement, but I also want the feed to be populated when people come to check us out. It's a delicate balance to strike.

I pause my work when it's time for Luca to place the railing and I hold the bottom of it for him while he gets the top into the position he wants it.

"I'm going to use these pins to hold it in place for now, and we can permanently affix it later. This way we can go on and get some pictures of the new railing, and I can work on the next thing," he tells me.

"Won't leaving it for later be a safety hazard?"

He shakes his head.

"The pins are part of the railing, and they'll slot into these holes here." He motions to the hole right next to him, then points in the tops of the posts that line the stairs. "Since those are vertical, guests won't be able to accidentally knock the railing off if they bump into it; you'd have to lift straight up. My guess is this was designed for someone who wanted to be able to change out the railing easily, or someone who decorated seasonally and figured it would be easier to just remove the top rather than work around it."

"Can we do that?"

"You want to just let the pins do their work? Yeah, I don't see why not. Removing the top piece will make decorating much easier."

God, I love the sound of the word 'easier.'

I walk him through the next year's worth of posts over lunch, glowing when he praises the work I've put into it. I'm not normally someone who seeks out praise—knowing I've done a job well is enough for me; and even in the bedroom I tend to gravitate more toward light degradation—but getting it from Luca has my cheeks flaming.

"I'd say I can see both your degree and Britney in these plans, but honestly, it's all you," Luca says, taking in my plans.

"What do you mean?"

"You've always been good at thinking in the long term like this. It's why I wasn't worried when I found out about the struggles at the inn. Most people would have had a shortsighted approach that got them deeper in the hole, but you've been thinking about long-term effectiveness this whole time, and you're setting yourself—and the inn—up for ongoing success once we're back on our feet."

"Oh." I hadn't thought about it like that, but he's right. So many people approach business by looking at what's directly in front of them, chasing trends and therefore never being able to fully catch up or plan ahead. But even as a kid, I always thought about the future I wanted, and what I needed to do now in order to achieve it. When it comes to my dreams, the journey only matters in that it gets me to my destination. Not that that seems to have worked out for me lately. "Thank you for saying that."

Luca shrugs. "It's just the truth."

"Still."

We get back to work soon after that, and I smile as I listen to the sound of a hammer pounding away while I focus on the business side of things. For the first time in a long time, I'm hopeful that we really can turn things around.

CHAPTER THREE

A WEEK LATER, I've launched our social media accounts. Weeks of planning have culminated in a strategy I'm very proud of. Our first few posts a combination of pictures and videos—mostly of Luca working. He's shirtless in half of them, because I'm not above (consensually) exploiting him for views, but I make sure to keep the Luca thirst traps as classy as possible. We do have a long-standing reputation to uphold, after all.

The following grows faster than I expected. It's not huge, by any means, but I worried we'd be stuck in the double digits for the first few weeks. Instead, it only takes three days for us to hit our first hundred.

"You're good at what you do," Luca chides one night over dinner, "of course you're growing a following."

By the end of the week, we have over a thousand followers on TikTok and almost as many on Instagram. The Facebook page is slower to grow, but I expected that. Still, I post diligently on that platform, too, making sure the content skews toward the older and more financially-established crowd. The followers on the other sites will help make us popular, and maybe convince influencers to do collabs with us if we ever find the money for that, but Facebook is more likely to translate into actual guests.

The Monday after we start all this, I'm proven right with our first booking. It's for a family trip, and their accommodations fell through last minute.

"You're in luck," I tell them. "We just finished up some renovations earlier than anticipated, so our books weren't open for those dates yet." It's mostly true. There *were* renovations, that just wasn't the reason for our lack of bookings. "We're wide open, and there's a chance you'll have the place to yourselves, though of course we can't guarantee that." I explain that since we weren't planning to be open yet, all of the food will be catered rather than made in-house. Mindy Corden, the woman coordinating everything for her family, is so grateful that we can accommodate them that she doesn't mind.

Good. Because it'll be a while before I can afford to have a chef on staff again. This booking will go a long way toward helping, especially since the "catering" will really be me calling in the huge favor my friend Gracie owes me after I drove three states away to move her home when she packed up her life for a job she knew she wasn't excited about and quit a week after getting there. I helped her pack her stuff back up and road-tripped home with her, both of us keeping our call on speaker the whole way so we could talk on the drive, and she has made a living as a cooking influencer since then.

"I'm making good on that favor you owe me." It isn't the first thing I say to her when she answers the phone, but it's close. "My ask is big enough that *I* might actually end up owing *you* after this." I explain that we'll need three meals a day for three days, for eleven people, and that I'll pay for all the supplies but can't afford to pay for her labor.

"Nope," she says, and my heart sinks.

"Gracie, please. I really need this."

"Oh, to be clear, I'm saying yes to the gig. I'm saying no to you owing me a favor. Because after I absolutely kill it, you're going to hire me as your chef and give me full creative control over the menu."

"Creative control within reason. We'll need a staple menu, but you can offer a special chef's choice selection. *If* I hire you on full-time," I hastily add. "We can treat this as an audition."

"Deal."

"Okay," I say. "Let's get through this booking first and then we'll talk about the future."

I decide not to decorate before the guests arrive—there's nothing Luca and I can think of that really screams *January*, and trying to come up with something will only stress us out. Because we're now on a time crunch, Luca pauses his work on the shed, which I feel bad about. His lease will end while the Cordens are here, and he won't be able to move straight into his new home.

He'll just have to take the room directly next to mine, tucked into the secret staff area at the back of the main building.

I definitely don't think about what it'll be like to have him so close every night. How easy it would be to bump into him half-clothes in the private hallway outside our rooms.

The sound of tires on the gravel out front pulls me back to the real world. Luca and I greet the Cordens with big smiles, and Mindy almost falls over herself thanking us for taking their booking.

"Oh, trust me, we're happy to have you," I assure her. "You're the perfect trial run for our renovations. Just let us know what you love, and anything that's not working out for you, and we'll be sure to adjust going forward. We want to make sure this is a place people love enough to come back to."

I run through the check-in protocol with them, reminding them that dinner will start at 6:00 pm. I handed Gracie the cash to cover the meal charges and told her to buy whatever ingredients she needs, and that if there's anything left over, she can keep it. The tentative menu she texted me has me certain the Cordens are going to love what she makes them.

I lead them to the rooms on the second floor, pausing when we get to the stairs. There's an ivy vine threaded through the banister, with little white fairy lights dotted through it. I haven't been this way since last night, so I didn't see it before now, but it's gorgeous. I know Luca and I decided not to decorate the banister, but I'm glad he did; it's absolutely perfect.

"Oh, that's lovely!" Mindy's mother exclaims. "I know we're not supposed to, but I just love English ivy; it's so beautiful. And those lights!" She presses her hand to her chest. "These are the kinds of touches you just don't get at those big chains. They probably all have fake snow everywhere. So generic."

Fake snow is one of the things Luca and I talked about, but we ultimately decided it wasn't worth it for just one family, even if they're large. Besides, it gets messy, especially with children around. We'd considered doing it for next year though, but now I'm not so sure.

Once the Cordens have been shown all their rooms, I leave them to choose who will be sleeping where, and make my way back behind the desk, texting Gracie to check in on food prep. She sends back a selfie of herself covered in flour and who knows what else, and I grimace at the state of the kitchen behind her. She'll clean it, I know she will, but it's been so long since I've seen the kitchen in use that I panic a little at sight of it.

And then I look at the picture again.

Because it's only now sinking in that *the kitchen is in use*. I wish I could text Aunt Brit so she could celebrate with me, but then I'd have to explain to her that it hasn't been in use and why I've been lying to her all this time.

Instead, I forward the picture to Luca, who's somewhere in the building, doing…something. I'm not sure what. As the owner of the establishment, I probably *should* know. But it's Luca; I trust him completely. And, as evidenced by the way he decorated the railing, I'm right to trust him.

The Cordens love the railing decoration. I know we said we wouldn't decorate, but it adds a great touch. The railing is perfect. I add an emoji to the text I'm drafting him, then press send. It's marked as delivered a second later, but though I check my phone multiple times over the next hour, the read receipt never pops up.

Yes, Luca is someone who has his read receipts on. I could *never*.

I'm deep into designing a graphic I want to post tomorrow when he sneaks up behind me, poking me in the side. I barely swallow down my shriek, and he laughs. I shove him playfully. "You can't do that when we have guests. Bloodcurdling screams are hardly going to make them want to come back."

"Fine." Luca rolls his eyes. "I'll limit all shocks and scares to October. We can brand it as a haunted experience."

He's joking, but it actually might be a good idea. My thoughts must be playing across my face, because Luca groans.

"Wren, no. I was kidding."

"I know. But hear me out." I throw out some ideas of things we could do to really stand out from our competitors, and by the end I can tell he's on board.

"Okay, fine. But only if I can build some of the haunts. Let me have some fun with this."

"Done."

He grins wickedly, and it does something to me. Carnally.

"Wait, no," I backtrack frantically. "Done within reason."

"Too late," Luca taunts, turning to leave.

"Within reason!" I yell after him. He holds up a thumbs down and keeps walking without looking back. "Within reason!" I repeat desperately. I'm laughing by the time he disappears, and Mindy turns the corner a second later.

"You two are so cute. How long have you been together?"

"Me and Luca? Oh, no, we're not. He's just…" What is he? My business partner? My best friend's brother? Basically family? But, like, family I lowkey want to fuck and it's okay because we're not actually related?

"Ah, yes." Mindy smiles knowingly. She's maybe five years older than me, but the look in her eye makes me feel like she's about to impart some motherly wisdom. Which makes sense— she *is* in fact a mother, after all. "Ted and I were *just* at one point, too." She waggles her eyebrows and I laugh despite the misunderstanding.

"No, he's…he's basically family. He's my best friend's brother. Her *twin* brother."

"And she wouldn't approve." Mindy nods sagely.

"No, she would, actually. At least, she would claim to. Went on a whole drunken rant about it in college, telling us we had her blessing. Totally unprompted."

"So what's stopping you? Do you think he doesn't reciprocate your feelings? Because I've only seen the two of you interact for, like, five minutes, but even I can tell the feelings are there. On both sides." She raises her eyebrows meaningfully.

"Because she had to get incredibly drunk to tell us she was okay with it. If she actually were, she would have been able to tell us sober. Besides, he's Luca. He's way too sweet for me." The words slip out before I can think about them, but just as she goes to ask what I mean, her family joins spills into the lobby, saving me from having to give my very-not-work-appropriate answer.

They head out for whatever activity they have planned, leaving me to think about all the reasons why I *know* Luca and I would never work.

CHAPTER FOUR

I LOVE SEX.

And look, I understand that using that as a justification for why I wouldn't be a good fit with a man sounds strange. A lot of people like sex, and the stereotypes say this fact would actually make men like me more (not that I put much stock in stereotypes in general).

But the thing is, it's not just sex I like; it's specifically kinky sex. And not just the stuff that used to be considered kinky but has made its way into the mainstream lately (although, let's be real, I like those things, too). No; I have kinks that make people say in a worried whisper "people are into that?"

And if I'm not specifically into something, I'm generally down to try.

It's my best-kept secret. Only Lucy and my college roommate Kristin know, and Kristin only knows because she walked in on me in a compromising situation once when she came home from her weekend trip a full day early. And Lucy knows because, well, Lucy knows everything. Except my stupid crush on her brother.

Amendment: she absolutely knows about the crush, we've just never explicitly discussed it aside from that one night when she drunkenly gave us her blessing.

So yeah, Lucy is aware that I was a member of a sex club in college, and I've summarized a couple of the erotica books I've read for her—and told her she should never read, because if she was blushing that hard over just a general overview there's no way she could handle actually reading them.

She doesn't know that I'm still a member of a sex club. It's a two-hour drive, so I don't go as often as I'd like, but it's always worth the drive. She'd be *shocked* to know who else frequents it, not that I'd ever tell her. I respect their privacy too much, even if the rules of the club didn't strictly forbid us from disclosing the names of other members.

Luca, of course, doesn't know anything about that side of me. I don't think he'd judge me for being into tentacles or monster-fucking, but I'm also pretty confident he would never in a million years want to be suspended in midair while being fucked from both ends by masked strangers, all while being watched by a room full of people he barely knows, who then finish on his latex-clad body.

For example.

If I sometimes imagine he's one of those masked strangers, well, the point of the masks is that it really could be anyone behind them, right?

And while I really don't think he'd just me for what I'm into, he certainly wouldn't have any interest in joining in. He'd turn redder than Lucy does when I talk about my books, and there's a very real chance he'd never be able to make eye contact with me again.

But god, I bet he'd blush so pretty for me if given the chance.

I'm still thinking about that when he returns from walking the Cordens out, and I have to fight to banish the dirty thoughts from my mind.

He drops down onto the stairs and watches me fiddle with the lights twined through the railing. They look perfect; I just need something to do with my hands while I try my best to avoid the train of thought Mindy's comment sent me down. But the longer I spend fiddling with this railing, the harder it is to turn my thoughts away from Luca. He's the one who found it and installed it. He's the one who decorated it.

Luca is like if the concept of competency porn came to life and wow, I'm wet just thinking about how he handled the whole railing situation and how I want him to handle *me.*

And maybe it's because I'm already letting my imagination run so wild, but I swear I feel the railing stiffening and pulsing in my hands, like a perfect erect dick.

Okay it's *definitely* because I'm letting my imagination run wild.

I close my eyes and fan my face with my hands in an attempt to cool down.

"Hey, are you feeling okay? You look flushed." He peers at me closely and presses the back of his hand against my cheek to check for a fever. It's cool from the January air and I lean into it, giving myself one moment to pretend this is something more than it is. "Oh, my hand is too cold to check. Here." He pulls me closer to him and presses the inside of his lips against my forehead in the open-mouthed kiss our parents always used to do to check for fevers when they couldn't find a thermometer.

It isn't a kiss.

It's just basic concern.

But my eyes flutter shut and I learn into him.

With all the things I've done with strangers, I never would have expected a simple non-kiss to make me melt like this.

He pulls away, declaring that my temperature is normal, but I know my cheeks are burning even hotter now. "Ohhhh," he teases, grinning. "I get it. You're not sick; you were thinking about having your way with me."

"Um." I clear my throat and his eyes go wide when I don't deny it. I scrabble for the denial that would normally be so quick on my tongue, but my mind is still blank with imagined pleasure.

Note to self: don't fantasize about my lifelong crush while basically giving a hand job to a thick piece of wood.

"Wait, really?" The smile drops from his face, and I swear his gaze darts to my lips for the briefest moment. "Wren, were you?"

His voice is anguished as he steps forward, and I genuinely can't tell if it's because he wants it just as much as I do, or because he really, really doesn't.

Thankfully, I'm spared from having to answer by Gracie calling my name from the kitchen. I flee, grateful for the excuse to run from this conversation that's both long overdue and should never happen, and I swear I hear him whisper my name as I scurry away without a backward glance.

"I need you to taste this," she urges, shoving a spoon at me. The soup is perfectly creamy, roasted red pepper with the tiniest hint of spice, and I give her a double thumbs up as she flings the spoon into the sink with a dramatic sigh. "One of the kids recognized me, so now this has to actually be good."

"It always had to be good," I remind her. "And it will be. It *is*. You're good at your job." I hang out with her while she finishes cooking, and by the time the Cordens come back, she's created a feast worthy of an establishment that charges a hell of a lot more than we do.

We throw on matching aprons and serve them, and the young girl who recognized her earlier squeals when Gracie serves her. "Oh my gosh, I'm, like, obsessed with you," she says. "I've watched all of your videos, and you inspired me to be a cook, too!"

"It's true," her mom says. "Hannah wants to make everything you make. She's become quite the cook. She handles dinner twice a week, now, all thanks to you."

"Wow, that's amazing!" Gracie tells. "Keep up the good work. I can't wait to try some of your cooking someday."

"Maybe we can cook together while we're here?" Hannah says hopefully.

Gracie crouches down so she's eye-level with the ten-year-old. "I'll show you the menu tomorrow and you can decide which meal you want to help with, how does that sound?"

"Oh my gosh, really? This is so great! I'm so excited! Mom, I'm going to cook with Gracie In The Kitchen!"

"That's so cool," her mom gushes. "Thank you so much, Gracie, you have no idea what this means to her."

Gracie shakes her head. "You have no idea what it means to *me*." She presses her hand to her chest and blinks tears from her eyes. "I'm really looking forward to it."

She pulls me back into the kitchen, and that's when she lets the tears actually fall. I hold her while she cries, and I'm holding back tears of my own by the time they finally slow enough for her to take a deep breath and speak.

"Thank you for this opportunity, Wren."

"I forced you into it," I say with a laugh. "It's not like I took a chance on you; I needed free labor, and I know you're fucking great at what you do. If anything, *I* should be thanking *you*."

"We can thank each other, then," she says.

"Perfect. And hey, when you have some free time, start thinking about what you might want the menu to look like."

I manage to avoid Luca for the rest of the evening, and I only feel a little bit guilty. I have too many thoughts and feelings swirling in my mind, and I want to try to wrangle them into something I can be coherent about before I talk to him. Because knowing him, he's not going to let me just pretend like our little moment earlier never happened.

I make sure the Cordens are all set for the night, then sit down to get some more work done. After a while I realize I haven't taken a picture of the railing with its new decorations yet, so I snap a few, then do some light editing on the photos to make sure they're up to my standards for the social media pages.

While I'm editing, I notice the light is creating a bit of an optical illusion with the railing, so it almost looks like it's moving between shots. I make a folder on my computer that I label *Halloween Inspo* and add the pictures, hoping they'll help me recreate the effect when we have the Halloween decorations up in October. We can make a little slideshow, or maybe edit the pictures together to make a little stop-motion video of the staircase coming to life.

When I'm satisfied with the photo and caption combo I've been working on and have it added to the queue to auto-post in a few days, I head to bed, trailing my hand along the curved base of the railing as I pass it.

I pause.

I swear it was curved the other way when Luca and I were setting it up. It was curved to the right, and now the swirl goes left.

I shake my head. Obviously, that must have been when I was holding it upside-down. The railing is all one big piece; there's no way this portion could have changed orientation. Still, I'm glad this is the direction it curves; it looks much better in the pictures this way.

I pass the stairs and take the hidden hallway that leads to the staff rooms. Aunt Brit initially intended to live up in the attic, but she realized she could charge more for the view up there, so she moved to the old storage room, sprucing up this whole section of the house that's tucked away behind the stairs. There are two bedrooms, each with their own bathroom, and I used to love staying here when the inn was too full for me to get a guest room of my own. When I took over ownership of the inn I thought I'd claim Aunt Brit's old room, but my old room held so much nostalgia I decided to take that one, even though it's slightly smaller.

There's a faint light coming from under the door of the other bedroom—*Luca's* bedroom for now—and I soften my footsteps so I don't alert him to my presence. I'm still not ready to face him after my almost-confession earlier.

But once I reach my room, I can't stop thinking about him in there. It's his first night sleeping at the inn, and I can practically feel his presence through the wall. I'm thinking about him when I slip into the shower, and when my hands drift between my legs. I slip two fingers inside myself—one in my cunt and the other in my ass—and imagine Luca watching me as I slowly finger myself. I need to be quiet, not wanting him to hear me.

But, of course, the thought of him hearing me turns me on.

I push my fingers deeper, faster, harder, picturing him listening in from his room. I don't need to imagine it's his fingers inside me; just the thought that he could hear my quiet gasps and low moans is enough to heighten the pleasure I feel.

I rub my thumb against my clit, using just enough pressure to make me buck with every pass, and I barely stop myself from calling out Luca's name when I finally come, sagging against the shower wall as wave after wave of my orgasm wrack through me.

I wash myself quickly after that and slip on my favorite pajamas: an old pair of leggings and a threadbare shirt that's impossibly soft. I expect to fall asleep quickly, but I lie on my back staring at the ceiling for long enough that I eventually give up and put on a show I've watched a thousand times.

CHAPTER FIVE

THERE SOFT KNOCK on my door around midnight isn't entirely unexpected, and I think about ignoring it and pretending to be asleep. Instead, I groan and drag myself out of bed. I guess it's time to avoid the conversation I manage to avoid all night.

I check the peephole in the door just to confirm my suspicion that it really is Luca before opening the door.

Luca is leaning against the opposite wall, and I can't quite make out the expression on his face as he takes in my outfit, and it's only under his scrutiny that I remember this shirt used to belong to him. Lucy grabbed it out of a donation pile in high school, then left it in my room in college, and I never gave it back to her.

I always forget it was his shirt before it was Lucy's, but in light of the conversation we didn't have earlier, I know how this must look.

He doesn't come inside or even say hello; he just stares at me with burning heat in his eyes, then slowly shakes his head. "Come with me. I want to show you something."

I pull the door closed behind me and fold my arms across my chest, fighting the urge to say anything; there's nothing I could say that would make this moment any less awkward.

"Where are we going?" I keep my voice low, despite the fact that our rooms are on the ground floor behind a closed heavy door, and the Cordens are all sound asleep a whole level above us.

He reaches out a hand like he's planning on taking mine, then stops, leaving it hovering in midair for a long, awkward beat before he abruptly turns and walks away. I follow, rushing to keep up with him. He isn't much taller than me, but he always walks with purpose, like he's late to wherever he's going, so he makes it halfway down the little hallway before I catch up with him.

We walk in silence through the building, out the back door and through the gardens that will start budding with new life in the next few months. I know where he's taking me before we arrive, but I still gasp at the sight of the pergola, strung with little white lights that match the ones on the staircase.

"I got the idea from the railing," he tells me, taking his usual seat on the left side of the bench swing. I slide in next to him.

"What do you mean?"

"The lights. They were a nice touch." He doesn't usually fish for compliments like this, but he's right, they were a nice touch, and I tell him so. "I know he agreed not to decorate," he continues, "but I think that should be our new January thing. Ivy and white lights."

"Definitely." I tuck my feet up under me, but don't lean my head on his shoulder like I normally would. I don't want to have to pull away for the tough part of this conversation, whether that's him rejecting me or me having to explain my...darker proclivities as proof of why we shouldn't be together.

"I've been thinking a lot about the night Lucy told us we should be together," Luca starts, looking up at the stars above us. "I know we both brushed it off at the time, but..." he fiddles with something in his hands. A small piece of wood, I realize—something he carved from the old railing. He holds it out to me and I take it, holding it up to the light.

It's small, about the width of my thumb and half the length. One side is mostly smooth, with thin ridges running through it. The other side has peaks and valleys.

It's a face.

More than that.

It's *my* face.

I hold it closer to one of the tiny lightbulbs, and the eye socket catches the light. The wood gleams, and though the light isn't particularly strong, it's clear this is a perfect rendering.

"Luca, this is…" I can't find the words, but I don't need to. He doesn't, either; this tiny carving, with its perfect attention to detail says everything. It would be impossible to carve this without it meaning something.

Without it meaning *everything*.

My heart sinks.

It would have been easier if he didn't reciprocate my feelings. Because how do you tell someone that you want to be with them, but that you won't?

"There's something I need to tell you," I whisper.

Luca angles himself toward me. His body is relaxed but I can see the trepidation in his face. He thinks I'm going to reject him. I'm not; I'm just going to hand him the ammunition he needs to reject me.

"I've thought about that night a lot, too," I start, my voice coming out shaky. It would be so easy to just say yes to his unasked question. To close the small gap between us and press my lips to his. To have one brief, shining moment where I know what it's like to kiss Luca Miller before I close that door forever.

"Yeah?" The smile that spreads across his face is soft and hopeful, and I close my eyes against it.

"But." I swallow, unable to form the next words. Beside me, he stiffens, and the bench swing rocks with his slight movement. "There's something I need to tell you. Something most people don't know about me."

"What is it?"

I turn the carving in my hand, trying to think of the best way to say it. It's the first time I've struggled with the phrasing. I love being kinky—I feel no shame around it, and by the time I'm discussing it with a partner I generally know they want it, too. I haven't kept this side of me secret because I'm embarrassed or think there's something wrong with my desires; I do it because it's usually irrelevant; I don't feel a particular need to discuss my sex life with anyone who isn't intimately involved.

"Wren?" he asks, and it's the worry in his voice that makes me just go for it. Because whatever he's picturing is probably worse than what I'm about to say, and I don't want him to panic.

"I'm into some really weird sex stuff, and I don't want to scare you away, but I think we're probably incompatible, so I never wanted to go for it with you even though I've fantasized about it, like, a whole lot." I rush through the words, unable to look at him as I say it. I don't want to face the disappointment as he realizes I'm right about us being incompatible.

"You've fantasized about it? About *me*?" he asks. I nod. "Doing what?"

"Sex. To me, specifically. *With* me. I don't know." I groan, covering my face with my hands. Luca gently pulls the carving from between my fingers then peels my hands away from my face.

"Tell me." There's a hunger in his eyes that I'm about to either fuel or douse entirely.

"Fucking me in the shower, for starters."

He laughs, and it's so full of delight that it spreads warmth through me, despite my best efforts to keep emotions out of this conversation. "That's not weird, Wren."

"While other people watch."

"Oh." He swallows hard, and when I risk a glance at him, I see that his pupils are blown out. "That—yes."

"Yes?" my voice comes out raspy as warmth floods between my legs. I picture him pressed against my back, his dick sliding inside me, one hand around my throat and the other pinching my nipple. And someone watching from the other side of the lightly-fogged glass.

"If I got to fuck you, I'd want the world to know."

"You want to claim me. You want everyone to know I'm yours." I barely dare to say the words aloud, and they come out as a whisper. The thought has me squirming, and he holds onto the post behind him to steady the bench as it begins to gently swing.

"No." His eyes dart down to my lips. "I want everyone to know that *I* am *yours*. God, Wren, I've spent half my life desperate to tell people that I belong to you."

I shouldn't be so turned on by that. He doesn't belong to me, and even if there were something between us, he'd still be his own person. But fuck if the thought of claiming him as mine doesn't make me moan. The sound is quiet, barely there, but he snaps his gaze to mine.

"What else? Tell me what you want, Wren." There's a note of desperation to his voice that makes me imagine him tied up and spread before me. So I tell him exactly that.

"I want to tie you up so you're completely at my mercy, then tease you for hours until you can't hold back and come all over yourself. Then I want to lick it off you." My breath hitches and I look away. I can't believe I just said that to him. To *Luca*. Not to some guy at a sex club who signed up for exactly this sort of thing. No; Luca is one of the sweetest, most innocent people I know.

But a second later his fingers are on my jaw, turning my face and forcing me to meet his gaze, which fucking *smolders*.

And then Luca's lips are on mine.

The kiss is desperate and hungry, and I sink into it, threading my fingers through his hair. I nip at his bottom lip and he moans, a low, guttural sound, and I straddle him without breaking the kiss. I roll my hips, grinding against him, desperate to press every part of my body against his. He's hard against my slick core, and even with all the layers of fabric between us, he feels incredible.

"Wren," Luca says urgently, pulling back. *"Wren."*

"Yeah?" I ask, dazed, my mouth swollen and my hips still rocking of their own accord.

"If you don't stop doing that I'm going to come."

"Good," I mumble against his lips. He groans, and his hips push up to meet mine thrust for thrust. He wraps his arms tighter around me, pulling me closer and grinding hard.

His dick pulses against me, and I suck the whimpers from his mouth as his orgasm floods his pants, soaking through the thin fabric of my leggings and mixing with my own wetness.

"Fuck, Wren," he whispers, pressing his forehead against mine.

I laugh weakly. "Yeah."

We stay like that for long minutes, catching our breath in the chill January night, until he presses a soft kiss to my lips. "We should actually talk, though. That was great, and I'd like to do more of it, but we should figure things out."

"Yeah." I shift to get off his lap, but he holds me tight.

"We can talk like this. If that's okay."

"More than." I lean forward to nestle my face in his neck.

"So, I think I can safely say that whatever you're into sexually, I can match that energy." His throat vibrates against my cheek as he speaks, and I lick it, eliciting a low moan. "Fuck, Wren."

I kiss the skin I just licked softly. "I'll be good now. Talking."

"I'm second-guessing the talking. There are better things we could be doing," Luca says.

"No, you're right. Talk now. Then better things later."

Luca chuckles. "Yes ma'am." A shiver runs through me. "Cards on the table," Luca says, and I turn my attention to the talk we're having with our words, instead of the one I want to be having with our bodies, "I think I've been in love with you pretty much my whole life." I suck in a sharp breath, and he runs his fingers up and down my back as he keeps talking. "I know that's a lot to lay on you, but I figured, since we're talking anyway, I don't want to hold back. Not after keeping this to myself for so long."

"Me, too," I whisper. "I've had this big, stupid crush on you forever. I've compared every guy in my life to you. I just didn't think we'd be compatible, so I never said anything. Because I don't want to lose you as a friend."

"You won't. Wait, why did you assume we wouldn't be compatible."

"Because you're so damn sweet," I mumble into his neck. "You're gentle and kind and you carry around a notebook that you sometimes write fucking *poetry* in. I figured you'd be into, like, missionary with the lights off or something."

"Don't get me wrong, I love missionary with the lights off. Give me a piece of ice to trail down your stomach, that you can't anticipate because you can't see it..." I shudder, and he laughs. "I could say the same for you. You're so focused and dedicated, and you have a spreadsheet for everything. I guess I kind of assumed that would extend to the bedroom."

"I do have a spreadsheet for the bedroom," I confess. "A few, actually."

"I can't tell if you're joking," Luca says.

"I'm not."

"And that's what I love about you." He presses a kiss to the top of my cheek, and I smile.

"I love you, too. I didn't say that before, but I do."

"So, what does this mean? Are we dating? Do you want to be my girlfriend? *Will* you be my girlfriend? Please? Fuck, what am I even saying? Let me try that again. Wren, perchance—fuck. Never mind." He slumps, defeated, and I shake with laughter.

"Perchance? *Perchance?* Let me take you out of your misery. You're my boyfriend now. Done. If you *ever* say perchance again, I'm breaking the fuck up with you."

CHAPTER SIX

THE REST OF THE CORDENS' trip goes off without a hitch. Hannah and Gracie make dinner together, and her mom signs a release for Gracie and the inn to use footage of the two of them cooking on our socials. After they leave, Gracie, Luca, and I sit down to talk about our next steps. Gracie's proposed menu looks great—a perfect blend of dependable staples that change daily and rotate through the seasons, plus a smaller menu that she has complete creative control over. We settle on the fee for anyone who wants to do a cooking class with her, with the money from that going directly to Gracie minus a 10% facilities fee.

More bookings slowly trickle in, but we have almost a week until our next guests arrive. It's slow, but it's the kind of momentum that makes me hopeful that we might finally be back on our feet.

Gracie leaves, and Luca and I find ourselves alone in the inn.

I don't have to ask if he's been anticipating this moment as much as I have; I've seen the excitement and need in his eyes all morning.

I lock the front door, even though it's been drilling into me from a young age that the inn should always be open. But as much as I love the fantasy of someone walking in to find us in a compromising position, I can't risk it. Not in my place of business, and certainly not with un-consenting witnesses.

When I turn around, Luca's eyes are on me, so hot I swear I'm going to combust.

I walk to him slowly, and with every step, my heart beats a little faster. Luca looks at me like he's ready to devour me, and though I expect him to meet me halfway, he just leans against the railing of the staircase, watching me with a sinful little smirk on his face.

When I get within touching distance, he hooks a finger under the belt at my waist and tugs me into him.

"You look fucking incredible today," he breathes against my mouth.

"So do you." His tight white shirt displays the muscles he's honed over years of manual labor. I want to rip it off of him.

Before I can do anything so bold, Luca spins us around and lifts me onto the thick swirl at the base of the railing. It feels wider than I remember, perfectly cradling my ass as Luca drops to his knees and hikes my legs over his shoulders.

He slides the fabric up my thighs so slowly that he has to be doing it specifically to heighten the anticipation. But I won't give in. Not yet. He's going to have to work harder than this if he wants to make me beg.

He glances up at me with a devilish glint in his eye, then digs his thumbs into the soft flesh of my thighs.

And then, a moment later, he dips his head and bites me. His bite is wide-mouthed, just the way I like: dull pain instead of a sharp sting. It lasts mere seconds, but I swear a lifetime passes in the span of that bite.

At the club, I'm known for being stoic. For making people work to pull even the slightest sound out of me. But Luca's teeth on my thigh and his hands on my thighs and ass feels divine, and I can't help but moan.

He chuckles, and the sound is deep and dark, so at odds with anything I've ever associated with him that it shocks me in the best way.

But it's more than that.

I've heard that chuckle before.

At the club, there's one man I like playing with the most. As far as I know, I've only interacted with him in the anonymous spaces, where everyone is masked or the lights are too low for anyone to make out identifying details. I've never seen his face, and none of the unmasked men have every fucked me quite in the way he does. But I know the feeling of his teeth, and the self-satisfied sounds he makes when he does something I clearly like.

The same teeth that just bit my inner thigh.

The same sound that just came out of Luca's mouth.

All this time I've been pining over Luca, and it turns out I've been fucking him for years.

"Luca." I breathe his name in wonder as I slide my hand into his hair and tug his head up.

"Hmm?"

"Come here."

He complies, kissing his way up my body. I arch into his lips, reveling in the sensation, even as a tiny part of me is sad at me realization. I've fantasized about threesomes with Luca and my favorite stranger, or one of them railing me while the other one watches, and now I know that can never happen.

But it does mean that even before I ever knowingly sleep with Luca, I already know he's the best sex of my life.

"What is it?" Luca has finally reached my face, and something about my expression must tip him off—but I see the realization dawn before I have a chance to respond. His eyes widen with shock, and then a slow smile stretches across his face. "Oh my god."

I can't help it; I laugh.

"No fucking way. Fuck, Wren. Really?"

I nod, fighting my laughter. "All these years wanting each other, and it turns out we were fucking the whole time."

"Oh my god," he says again. This time, he laughs, too. "I mean, it wasn't the whole time. I've been wanting you for way longer than that. But yeah. If only one of us had figured it out sooner, we'd have saved *years* of pining."

"Mmm. I kind of like that we didn't know. The fantasies I've had about the two of you…" I trail off and raise my brows at Luca, daring him to ask.

Instead, he steps closer, pressing between my thighs. And oh, I can feel exactly what he thinks about that. I cant my hips forward, drawing our bodies flush, and he flexes his hips against me.

"Tell me," he whispers against my lips. His hands slide up my calves and my thighs, when around to cup my ass. "Tell me the fantasies you had about the two of us. Tell me all the ways you want me to fuck you."

I open my mouth to tell him, but he kisses me before I can get a single word out. "You're in such a rush," he admonishes. "Let me get into position, first."

Without breaking eye contact, Luca drops to his knees on the stairs in front of me. Then, with a saucy grin, he ducks his head underneath my skirt and bites my inner thigh again.

I buck against him, but my skirt catches on the railing, holding me in place. No matter how hard I strain, I can't move enough to press myself against his face.

I move a hand to try to free myself, but I must accidentally slide it inside the groove of the railing's swoop, because my hand gets caught, holding me even more firmly in place. I struggle for a few seconds before deciding to let it go—I do love being bound, after all. Even if this time it's accidental, it's still hot.

Luca bites his way up my inner thigh, probably leaving a trail of light bruises, until he finally reaches my cunt. He eats me like a starving man while I writhe against his face, almost fully immobilized by the railing.

My orgasm rips through me hard and fast and I come, shaking, against his face. He stands and grins at me with his mouth and chin glistening, and when he leans in for a kiss, I drag my tongue down his chin instead.

I slide a hand into his hair to pull him closer, and only then do I realize I've managed to free my hand from the railing.

Luca grabs my underwear off the stairs, but when I reach out my hand for them, he shakes his head. Then, with a devilish wink, he puts them in his pocket.

I slide off the banister and go to lead Luca to our rooms—but there's a jerk against my hand. I whirl around to find him stuck just like I was, his shirt caught in the curl of the wood.

"We should make sure this doesn't happen to the guests." So far, the only two people to get caught on the railing are us, and only while engaging in sex acts on the stairs, but still. We wouldn't want to risk upsetting guests with a wayward railing.

Luca nod and tries to free himself, but I have a better idea.

I grab his hands and turn him, walking him up a step as I twist his hands behind his back and rest them on the railing.

"Stay," I command. I trail my hand down the broad plane of his chest, slowly lowering myself until I'm seated on one of the steps, leaving my face level with the massive erection straining his jeans. Luca groans, and I run a single finger down the bulge in his pants. "I think it's my turn," I murmur. "After all, I've never seen your dick knowing it was *your* dick. Don't you think that's long overdue?"

Luca nods fast, breathing hard, and I chuckle darkly. "Should I tease you?" I ask, running my fingers up one thigh, across his stomach, and down the other. "Or should I touch you?" I ask, palming him through his jeans. He bucks against my palm as I give a gentle squeeze.

"Yes," he breathes.

I undo the buckle of his belt and slowly pull it through the belt loops, drawing out the moment as long as I can before I finally pop the button of his jeans and grip the zipper between my fingers. I draw it down as slowly as I possibly can, and Luca is trembling in my hands by the time I'm done.

His erection springs free, tenting his black boxer briefs, and I press my nose against it, inhaling deeply. I smell musk and a hint of salt, and I suddenly want nothing more than to taste him. I yank his underwear down roughly, taking a moment to admire him. His dick is thick and slightly darker than the rest of him, jutting out from a patch of black hair.

He curses when I take him into my mouth, and stays perfectly still, not even slightly shifting his hips as I slowly take him inch my inch, until my nose is buried in the curls at the base of his shaft and my throat stretches around his dick.

I draw back and look up at him. He's gazing down at me in awe. "You—"

"Don't have a gag reflex," I smirk. He's experienced it before, but I can tell from the look in his eyes that he hadn't fully processed it until this moment.

"Fuck," he breathes.

"That comes later. For now—" I take him all the way in one shift motion, and he bucks against me, pushing his dick against the back of my throat. I moan around him and he groans, jerking against me.

It isn't long before he's warning me that he's going to come. I appreciate it, but I don't pull back, and when he comes in my mouth, I swallow every salty drop.

"God, Wren, that was—" he stops, his eyes going wide. "I'm stuck."

I rest my head against his bare thigh. "I know. That's how we got in this position."

"No, I'm *more* stuck now. My hands." There's panic in his voice and I bolt upright. Somehow, his hands have slipped through the opening in the curve of the railing. What are the chances that this has happened to both of us, especially since nobody's gotten stuck before today?

I run around to the other side and carefully start working his hands free.

I'm halfway through when the wood moves.

It *moves*, fully of its own accord, and releases his hands.

"What the fuck?"

"What?" Luca asks, turning now that his hands are free.

"The wood just fucking moved."

"What—" he cuts off with a sharp gasp as we both watch the wood form itself back into its original shape. He hurriedly pulls his pants up as we bend to examine the railing together. "It just *moved*." He runs a hand through his hair. "That's impossible."

"And yet..."

We stare at each other in shocked horror as the wood continues to slowly twist and curl.

"I mean, we could lean into this and bill the inn as haunted." It's a weak joke, and I don't blame him one bit when he ignores me in favor of trying to find an answer. He examines it closely, running a finger down the smooth grain of the wood, and I swear it shivers in response.

Luca leaps back, and we run across the room to the front desk.

"I'm kind of freaked out," he admits a few minutes later. We're both leaning against the desk and eyeing the railing warily. It hasn't stopped moving, but it's made no move to come toward us. It's like it doesn't realize we're still here.

Of course it doesn't. It's a fucking piece of wood. It can't *realize* anything.

"Me, too. It would help if we knew what was happening. I'm just glad you saw it, too."

"Yeah," Luca agrees. "Imagine if only one of us saw it. I would have thought you were making it up. Or hallucinating."

"Believe me, I haven't ruled it out." Something's going on, and it can't be that the wood is actually moving on its own; that's simply not how the laws of physics work. A sudden reck-lessness overtakes me, and I stalk across the room and poke the railing. "What's going on with you? How did you do that?" I don't actually expect an answer, obviously.

I *definitely* don't expect the railing to uncurl slowly, like a sprout emerging from a seed.

Luca darts forward, grabs me around the waist, and hauls me

backward as the railing continues to straighten. It bends forward, sliding down the banister until it lays across the floor like a large wooden snake. And then, it slowly creeps toward a black lump on the floor—my underwear, which must have fallen out of Luca's pocket. It hooks through one of the leg holes and lifts it from the ground, slowly reaching toward us.

I recoil, but Luca stays perfectly still as the railing gets closer. He extends a shaking hand to grab the garment, and as soon as he does, the railing retreats.

"Thank you?" he says hesitantly. The railing bobs like its' nodding, then takes its usual place on the banister. The end curls back the way it was before all this started, and it looks for all the world like a normal fucking railing.

"Well, I think it's safe to say we need a heavy meal and a whole lot of alcohol after that," I declare, pulling Luca into the kitchen and directing him to the stool Gracie sometimes sits on while she chops.

We don't talk while I whip up some food, or while we eat.

It's only after he finishes eating that Luca says a hesitant "So…"

"So," I agree.

"What the fuck was that?" The bewilderment in his voice matches mine.

"Well," I say slowly. "If I believed in the supernatural, I would say that the railing is haunted. If we'd eaten mushrooms we foraged, I would say we were tripping or experiencing some sort of group psychosis. But…"

"But," he agrees. "That happened. It actually, really happened."

"Yeah." I drop my head onto the counter. "It actually, really happened."

"The railing bound me while you went down on me." Luca shifts in his seat. "Is it weird to say that you going down on me is almost the most unbelievable part of that?"

"No, it's not. What?"

"I've dreamed of that for *years*, Wren. Pretty much the second I found out what a blowjob was, I imagined you giving me one. Well," he amends, "the second I realized that they could actually be fun. When I first found out about them, I was kind of horrified at the thought of having my dick in someone's mouth."

I laugh, and feel some of the tension melt away. "Right? It's kind of a weird concept, if you think about it. I thought the kids who told me and Lucy about them were lying. I was like 'oh my god, I'm not going to fall for that, obviously nobody would ever do that.' And now here I am, eating an astonishing amount of crow."

"Actually, I take it back. The most unbelievable part is that we've been doing that for years and never knew. I can't believe we never figured it out."

"To be fair, I could have looked right into your unmasked face and I still wouldn't have believed it was you in the club," I tell him. Luca shakes his head ruefully.

"I can't believe you thought I was that…what, innocent?"

I shrug. "You give off a vibe. Besides, I had to believe it to quash the rampant fantasies running through my mind."

"*Rampant* fantasies?" Luca groans and pulls me into him, kissing me hard and I melt into the kiss.

"Okay, we need to move. We don't need a health code violation on our hands," I say once the kiss starts heating up and hands are roaming places they absolutely shouldn't in what it technically a commercial kitchen. I pull his shirt over his head to punctuate the need to find another place to do this and he nods, standing and grabbing my hand. He pulls me back into him the moment we're out of the kitchen, and I wiggle my ass against the thick bulge in his pants.

"Wren," he groans. I take a step back, laughing when he pouts, and pull my shirt over my head. His eyes drop to my chest and widen as I unclasp my bra, freeing my breasts. He gazes at them hungrily before reaching out and gently cupping them both. He drops his head to take one of my nipples into his mouth, lightly scraping his teeth against it, and I let out the filthiest moan as pleasure shoots through me.

I fumble with his pants. A moment later they're on the ground and I have his perfect dick in my hand again.

He surges up and catches my mouth in his again. "Not yet. I want to play with you some more first." But he flexes his hips, pushing his dick into my fist and dropping his head onto my shoulder. I squeeze harder, then let go.

"Not yet? You sure about that?" I'm teasing, and based on our encounters in the club, I expect him to change his mind, maybe even to beg me to touch him again. But he just nods, capturing my mouth in another kiss and biting my bottom lip.

"Bed," he says urgently, and we don't break the kiss as we move.

We make it back to the base of the stairs and it isn't until my back bumps against the railing that I give it a second thought. I break the kiss. "What did it feel like, when it was holding your arms behind your back?"

"Why?" Luca asks from behind me, his breath tickling my ear. "Do you want to feel it for yourself?"

"I already did." I quickly explain how my skirt got caught and my hands bound while he was going down on me. I didn't realize at the time that the railing itself was actively holding me captive for him.

I nod, and he hardens against my back. "Fuck. Really? You want the railing to tie you up? Immobilize you so you're fully at my mercy?" The pure need in his voice makes my clit throb.

"I want a lot, Luca," I say, grinding my ass against him, and smiling when he moans. "You know I'm game for anything you want."

He slips a hand down the front of my skirt, groaning when his fingers find the slickness between my legs. "Wren," he whispers. "Close your eyes. I want you to picture this inn full of guests, and all of them are watching me touch you. All of them can see how bad you want this. Every hitch of your breath, every purse of your lips—it's all being watched by dozens of people."

I shiver against him, picturing it in my mind. He's an expert with his fingers, circling my clit to tease me, then rubbing it gently enough that I buck against his hand in a silent plea to go harder.

"No, love. We do this on my terms. You don't come until I let you."

Fuck.

I moan, nodding against his chest, and he rumbles a quiet laugh. "Good girl," he murmurs. "You're so wet for me. So fucking beautiful, too, you know that? What would make this better for you? I'll find an audience so everyone can see how fucking gorgeous you look when you come. And what about another person to play with us? To lick you clean so you don't get too wet while I tease you?"

I buck at that, my mouth falling open as I breathe "Yes."

"I need this off, love." He pulls my skirt off, leaving me standing in only my underwear.

"Wren." His voice is firmer now, more serious. Not enough to make me open my eyes and end the fantasy, but enough that I know I need to pay attention to whatever he says next, especially because his fingers have stilled against me.

"You said you want to be bound. By the railing?"

"By anything."

"Now?"

"Yes. Please," I whine.

"You're sure?"

"I'm sure." I rock my hips forward slightly, and he keeps playing with my clit as something winds against my wrists. It's hard and smooth, and even though he just asked me about it, it takes me a few seconds to realize it's the railing.

It caresses my wrists and stomach, barely-there pressure that deepens into something more intentional. It should be shocking.

Uncomfortable, even. But the wood is perfectly polished and smooth, and it's tantalizing against my bare skin.

Luca pulls me flush against him, his dick slipping between my legs, rubbing against my slick cunt, and a bead of precum drips down my inner thigh, warm and slick. He thrusts, his hips pressed hard against my ass, and the combination of his dick and his fingers brings me closer to orgasm than I have any right to be.

"Fuck," I gasp. "That feels—fuck."

"I know, baby. I know. It's so fucking good. You feel so fucking good. Oh, god," he whispers, pulling me somehow even closer.

Except, it isn't *him* pulling me closer.

The railing has wound itself fully around me—around *us*.

I'm bound to him by the wood curled around our legs, abdomens, and chests. It's just tight enough that I don't think I could put any space between us if I tried—not that I want to. I've never been bound *to* someone like this before. I don't know why I've never thought of it.

It's fucking hot as hell.

Behind me, Luca tries to thrust, but he can only move just enough to drag his dick against my clit. I gasp, shifting to squeeze my thighs around him.

The moan he lets out shoots straight to my pussy. My orgasm rips through me hard and fast, and I feel Luca's abs tense against my back as I jerk against him.

His left hand tightens on my hip and the fingers of his other hand trail across the patch of hair at the apex of my thighs, gently rubbing, coaxing me through the most powerful orgasm of my life.

"Fuck, Wren, I'm—" A moment later, Luca tenses against me, his abs flexing and his hips jerking against my ass. His cum paints the stairs in streaks of white, shooting way farther than I would have thought possible. The last few spurts trickle down my thighs, and I squirm at the sensation. I've dreamed of being covered in Luca's come for years, not knowing that I already have been. But this first time knowing it's him is every bit as hot as I fantasized it would be.

I want more later, want his cum on every inch of me, but for now I slump against him, thankful that the railing is holding us up, because I honest to god don't think I'm capable of standing on my own right now.

CHAPTER SEVEN

I WAKE up the next morning to sunlight streaming through my window and Luca's arm slung over my stomach. He radiates delicious heat, and I snuggle into him, relishing this moment. This part of the inn doesn't have the best airflow with the HVAC system, so I'm definitely grateful for the heat Luca throws off on this cold morning. Normally I would just add another blanket or two to my bed, but this is definitely preferable.

My stirring must have woken him, because a moment later he smiles up at me without even opening his eyes. "Morning, beautiful."

"You don't know I'm beautiful. Maybe I turn into a troll at night."

"An ogre," he mumbles, and I shove him playfully, but he only tightens his arms around me and scowls with his eyes still closed. "If you're going to reference Shrek, at least get it right."

"Maybe I wasn't referencing Shrek."

At that, he cracks a single sleepy, but thoroughly unamused eye at me. "Wren. Do you know how many times I've had to deal with you incorrectly referencing that movie? Like the time you called yourself garlic because some boy at school said you were boring and you wanted him to know you had layers? And that's just one of literally a thousand examples. You were absolutely referencing Shrek. And doing it badly."

"Fine," I mumble. "You do a better job, then."

And he does. He breaks into an absolutely perfect rendition

of that song the puppets sing outside of Dulcolax, or whatever the town is called.

I have never laughed so hard this early in the morning, and by the time we actually drag ourselves out of bed my heart is whispering that I could have this forever.

It's too early to be thinking like that, but...it's Luca. I've always dreamed about forever, even if I wouldn't admit it to myself.

We make scrambled eggs and toast in the staff kitchenette, and we eat it on the swing in the backyard, less clothed than we probably should be considering this is a place of business.

My place of business.

Our place of business.

"I know it's probably too early to be asking this," Luca says once he's done with his food, "but..."

He trails off, but I know exactly what he was going to say. I've been thinking about it this morning, too. She said she was fine with the thought of us together, but that was a drunken statement years ago, and it wasn't a particularly believable one. "What will Lucy think about her best friend and her brother being together?" I finish for him, grimacing as I voice the question aloud.

"Yeah. I know she said she'd be fine with it, but I don't know that I believed her."

"Yeah." I sigh. "I definitely didn't. It's part of why I never made a move."

"That and you thought I couldn't keep up with you in bed." He nudges me, and I laugh.

"You come across as incredibly vanilla! Which is not a bad thing, but it's just very much not *my* thing."

"It's not my thing, either." He presses a kiss to my cheek. "Unless you told me very sternly that it needed to be my thing for a while. Ideally with some physical reinforcement. Then it would very much be my thing." His voice has gone husky and sultry, and I shiver.

"Speaking of vanilla, and…physical reinforcement…"

He looks up at me from between his gorgeous, thick lashes.

"The railing…"

"Are you trying to process what happened yesterday or proposing we take this inside?"

"Yes."

"The railing really did it for you, huh?" There's enough heat in his voice that it's as much a confession as a question, and I simply bite my lip in response. "Come on." He takes my hand and pulls me to standing.

I think he's going to lead me straight to the staircase, but he pauses to grab both of our plates, and detours to the kitchenette, where he loads them both into the tiny dishwasher. And honestly, the only thing hotter than a man being desperate to worship you is a man stopping to do very light housework when he is desperate to worship you.

With the dishes safely in the dishwasher, Luca cups my face and slowly trails kisses down my next, lighting my every nerve on fire. "So, about that railing…"

"Oh, we'll be getting railed." I slip from his grasp and run down the hall.

"Both of us?" he calls after me.

"Yep!" I yell over my shoulder. "Up to you exactly what that means."

He catches up to me a second later, wrapping his arms around me and continuing to run. It's awkward and clumsy, and I'm laughing by the time we reach the stairs.

But just as he presses me against the wall, the front doorbell rings.

"Oh. Shit. There's people." I look down at my clothes, which are definitely not professional enough to greet guests. Luca and I glance at each other for one wide-eyed second before we sprint back to the staff quarters. I throw on the first dress I can find and throw my hair into a quick messy bun that I only hope passes for professional.

I make it to the door in less than a minute, and I'm probably prouder of myself than I should be. I take a second to compose myself, then open the door with as much grace as I can muster.

"Welcome to the Sunnyside Inn! I'm Wren, how may I help you?" My voice is remarkably steady, considering.

The couple at the door looks at me with hopeful desperation in their eyes.

"Hi, I'm so sorry," the woman says with a sweet southern drawl. "We're in town for a few days, but we're not happy at the place we've been staying, and I saw your Instagram page and absolutely fell in love. Please tell me you haven't booked up yet."

"You're in luck," I tell her, stepping aside so she and her partner can come inside. "Our bookings start up in earnest next week. Our renovations finished up earlier than expected, so we've got a few secret days on the books. For right now, you'll have the place to yourselves."

"Oh, thank the lord," she says, wrapping me in a heartfelt hug.

I get them checked in—Poppy and George Bellmont—and give them their pick of rooms, since it's just them.

Luca carries their bags to their room upstairs, and he throws me saucy glances behind Bellmonts' backs the whole way there.

As soon as they're settled in, I run to my room so there's no chance of them overhearing, and call Gracie.

"We have guests. Please tell me you can cook. On the premises or something dropped off, I don't care."

"Oooh, that's a good idea. Yes, I'm free. But also, I'll make up some frozen meals so you can reheat them if I'm ever not around."

"I fucking adore you, Gracie Adair."

"I know."

Within the hour, Gracie is in the kitchen, prepping meals for the next few days.

With the food handled, it seems like we'll have a nice quiet couple of days with the Bellmonts.

I couldn't be more wrong.

In the best possible way.

Poppy is apparently a pretty big deal in her social circles (both in person and online, from what George tells me—and a quick look at her socials confirms her *millions* of followers), and when she posts pictures of the inn with a caption about how we saved her, the bookings start pouring in almost faster than I can keep up with. We're still not up to heyday numbers—it'll be a while until we're booking three years out—but overnight we go from having an empty inn with only a handful of future bookings to being booked solid.

In the next eleven months, we don't have more than 3 days in a row without a booking. All thanks to Poppy.

It feels good. It's nice to look at the schedule and see so many names.

Plus, next time Aunt Brit calls, I won't have to lie to her about how well things are going.

Luca and I don't find time alone together until later that night. He ties me up and teases me for hours, so by the time I come on his tongue I'm a writhing, desperate mess. I can't even beg; he gagged me to make sure I didn't make too much noise while we have guests.

Over the next few days, Luca and I quickly learn that we can't be in the same room while there are guests at the inn. We both get way too distracted by the other person's presence, and on more than one occasion I've lost my train of through midway through a sentence with a guest because Luca flexed, or made eye contact with me.

Or because I smelled the heady mix of his sweat and cologne.

The good news is, this means we're both incredibly productive. Luca does handywork I didn't even realize needed to be done, and I plan, create, and schedule posts far farther out than I ever thought I would. I reach out to local businesses to ask them to recommend us, take out ads with the little profit we have coming in, and spruce up the entryway.

Unfortunately, Luca's not the only one I have to avoid.

I can't so much as look at the railing without reliving the way it bound me to Luca. Even worse, the railing seems to know this. Every time I walk past, it's in a slightly different position. When there's nobody else around, it waves to me from across the room. And when I walk the staircase, I usually feel the ghosting touch of wood against my handle, or a gentle tug on the hem of my clothes.

The railing is teasing me, and there's nothing I can do about it but blush.

But teasing me isn't the only thing the railing does; it adds lights to the ivy twined through it, and on the Bellmonts' second day, it adds a poinsettia at its base. Poppy coos over my attention to detail, and the amount of work I put into decorating the space.

After they're safely in bed for the night I linger at the bottom of the stairs. I run my fingers along the smooth wood, and it shivers in response.

"Thank you. You're making this place look really good. I'm getting all the credit, but you're the one doing it, and I just want you to know I appreciate it."

Maybe it should feel weird talking to a piece of wood like this, but after having a literal threesome with the railing, I think I can handle some light conversation.

By the time the Bellmonts leave, the inn almost looks like it did in my childhood: grand and beautiful, the kind of place you'd visit once and fall in love with, then plan entire vacations around because you're just that desperate to go back.

We have one full day between the Bellmonts leaving and our next few groups of guests arriving, and I intend to take full advantage of the alone time with Luca.

Unfortunately, I fail to notice Gracie exiting the kitchen when I draw Luca in for a lingering kiss in the dining room.

It isn't until she clears her throat that I even notice she's there. Luca and I jump apart guiltily. He looks between the two of us, and I shoo him away. Gracie will be much easier to deal with if Luca isn't here for this conversation.

The moment he disappears through the dining room doors, Gracie shoots me a knowing smirk.

"Careful, or you two are going to burn this place down with all the heat between you. Don't think I haven't noticed the tension before now, either. I don't know how new this is, but that certainly wasn't a first kiss I just witnessed." She raises her brows in mock warning. I shove her shoulder and she stumbles back dramatically with a faux-outraged gasp. "Okay, but really though. What's going on between you two? A fling? A relationship? What?"

"Yes."

Gracie laughs. "So we haven't had a conversation about things yet. Got it."

"No, it's not that. It's just…complicated."

"So you *have* had a conversation. Where'd you land?"

"On the fact that we work together and he's my best friend's twin brother, and we grew up together, and there's a lot riding on this, so we don't want to mess anything up."

"Especially because you're in love with him and can't stand the thought of potentially losing him."

"That too, yeah. But I'm less worried about that than I expected. Things are…good." I try to fight the smile that spreads across my face, but I can't; I'm just too happy.

"Damn." Gracie gapes at me. "I thought you'd deny the whole being in love with him thing."

"Nope." I shrug. "I've been denying it, including to myself, for years now. I'm done with that now. I love him, pure and simple, and I'm letting myself fully feel things."

"And how do things feel?" She waggles her eyebrows at me, making it clear *exactly* what she's asking about, and I blush. Which is frankly unlike me.

"Things feel really good," I whisper. I'm honestly not even sure whether I'm talking about Luca's dick, the conversations we have long into the night and the way he gazes at me in the morning, or the railing. Or just…life in general, right now. After years of feeling like I'm slowly drowning, the past few weeks have been a much-needed breath of fresh air.

"So," Luca says, dropping into bed beside me that night. He hasn't spent the night in his own room since the first time we slept together, and I've gotten used to him in my bed before we part for the day. "You've really turned this place around. It's incredible to witness."

"*We've* turned it around," I correct him. "I couldn't have done it without your help. All the work you've put into it. Not to mention you put me in a good mood every morning."

"Mmmm." He kisses me deep and slow, and I nestle into him. "I do love when you're in a good mood."

"It's a joint effort." I press kiss to his shoulder. When he doesn't immediately agree, I prompt him to. "You know it's a joint effort. Say it."

"Fine. It's a joint effort."

My phone buzzes, and I turn over to silence the incoming call, but I stop at the name that flashes across the screen.

"Who is it?" Luca asks.

"Lucy."

We both fall silent for a few seconds while the phone vibrates between us. Then, he voices the question on my mind: "Is it time?"

I swallow hard. I think it might be. I answer, glad that she didn't video call me. It's always a toss-up which it'll be, with her.

"Hey," she says brightly. "Are you busy?"

"No, what's up?"

"Just wanted to check in. I know we've been texting, but that's not the same as hearing your voice. Tell me everything about your life right now, go."

"Um. Well. First of all…" I trail off, and Lucy shrieks.

"Wren Elaine Thompson! Who is he?"

"How did you know there's a guy?!"

"I didn't!" Lucy yells. "Oh my god, please tell me everything. Every little detail. I want to live vicariously through you."

Luca lets out a strangled sound, and I throw my pillow at him.

"Oh my god," Lucy continues. "Is he into freaky shit? Please tell me you're living your best freaky little life with him. I know I only know, like, a small fraction of the stuff you're into, but please tell me this guy is doing absolutely depraved things—"

"Luce, I need to you stop talking right the fuck now!" I practically yell the words in desperation.

"Oh." The one syllable is quiet. I can't tell if she's suspicious or hurt. "Why?"

"You don't want those details this time. Trust me."

There's a beat of silence, during which I bite my lip as my heart races. I can't decide if I want her to come to the right conclusion on her own, or if I'd rather be the one to tell her. Neither seems like an ideal option, if I'm being honest.

Luca takes me free hand under the covers, and I wonder if he's as nervous as I am.

"Oh my god. Oh my *god*, Wren. Are you fucking my brother?!"

"Yes, I'm so sorry, I know I should have talked to you about it first but it just kind of happened and it's been really great and oh my god I am so sorry please don't be mad at me do you hate me now?" My words come out a jumbled mess, and Luca tenses beside me.

I can practically hear her wrinkling her nose through the phone.

"Why would I be mad?"

"Because he's your bother?"

"I literally told you back in college that I thought you two should get together! Neither of you ever brought it up so I just figured you both weren't interested, but you've had my blessing for ages."

"We didn't think you meant it," Luca says from beside me.

You seemed like you were actually upset about it and just trying to convince us and yourself that you were okay with it."

"Luca?!" Lucy screams. "Here's there? You're there? Are you fucking *right now?!*"

"Jesus, no, Lucy, what the fuck," Luca says, right when I say "Obviously, literally right this second. I always fuck while I'm on the phone."

There's a beat of silence, and then all three of us burst into laughter together.

"So you're really okay with this?" Luca asks.

"My best friend and my brother getting together? I literally couldn't have asked for anything better. You're so well suited to each other. And I like and trust you both. I only want the best for my best friend, and my brother is the best. And I only want the best for my brother, and my best friend is the best. Wow, that was a lot of bests," Lucy laughs. "I've been waiting for this to happen for *years*. Why now? What made it finally happen?"

We give her the abridged version. We're all in agreement that she doesn't need any of the details of her twin brother's sex life.

By the time we hang up I'm practically glowing with happiness.

Luca pulls me in close and presses a kiss to the top of my head. "That went surprisingly well."

"Yeah."

"Now we just have to tell her about the railing."

CHAPTER EIGHT

A MONTH LATER, I almost wish the inn weren't doing as well as it is.

I genuinely didn't think things would pick up this quickly, and we don't have the staff to make it work without logistics being a massive headache. Gracie has already enlisted help in the kitchen, but the two cooks she's hired are on her payroll, not ours, and that needs to be fixed as soon as possible.

When Aunt Brit calls, I tell her I'll have to call her back later; there are too many things for me to do, including hiring Gracie's cooks, and daytime and overnight managers so I can focus on the socials, which are now taking up all of my time.

"How about that visit?" she asks me before I can hang up.

"Yes! Soon. Let's talk tomorrow and we can get that scheduled. It would be really great to have you. And we'll have to see where I can fit you in; we're booked up pretty full."

"Ooh, so fancy. I'll just go online and make an appointment like a normal person, then."

I freeze. It never even occurred to me that she would do that, and now I wonder if she's checked the website before and realized we had way too many vacancies. I doubt it; she's never been good at technology. I'm honestly surprise she even knows we do online bookings.

"No need! I was just joking. Luca's been staying in your old room, but I can kick him out when you're here. Or you can stay in my old room. Whichever you'd prefer."

I'm so busy the next couple days that I forget to call her back until the weekend. And I'm frazzled when I do. "Okay, Aunt Brit, I've got about ten minutes. I have the schedule in front of me. Let's do this."

She decides to come home for her birthday, which is only three months away, and things are going so well I'm not even nervous about her seeing the place. She's going to be impressed, and with good reason; we've done great work here. I just need to make sure that we're properly staffed by then.

The week before Aunt Brit's visit, we finally secure out final (for now) staff member. We have enough people on payroll that I can actually take the occasional break again, which is much needed—I've worked over two months without a full day off, and it's starting to take a toll on me. Aunt Brit calls to say my parents are going to join her, and that they'll make do with whatever local accommodation they can find. But I tell her there's no need—Luca has gotten the shed into good enough shape that he's moved his things out there, and I'll just stay back there with him. Aunt Brit can have her old room, and my parents can have mine.

I've just finished moving a week's worth of clothes into the shed when my phone buzzes in my pocket. Assuming it's Aunt Brit or my parents with a trip update, I answer without checking who it is.

"Can I come stay with you next week? I'll be in town for a few days, and I know you probably don't have space for me, but I was hoping I could just crash in your room with you? Please, please, please?" Lucy's voice is so loud I wince and pull the phone away from my ear.

"You know you can always stay with me," I assure her. "You're in luck, we just got a cancellation this morning. It's for the room you hate, but it's the only one open."

"How much? I'll pay you right now."

"Lucifer, don't you even think about paying me for the room. Family doesn't pay here, you know that."

"I'm not family."

"That's a damn lie and you know it. You've *always* been my family."

"And maybe soon we'll legally be family, too," she taunts

"Oh my god, Luce, your brother and I have been together for like three seconds, it is *way* too early to start talking marriage."

"But you've thought about it," she says knowingly.

"Goodbye, Lucy."

"Wait—"

I hang up on her. If she has something important to say, she'll call me back or text me.

She does neither.

In all the whirlwind of the sudden full bookings and preparations for my family, there isn't much time for me and Luca to be alone with the railing together.

Even separately, it's hard to find the time.

I try to make sure to at least touch it when I walk past, but it's not enough. Even when Luca and I tumble into bed together at the end of a long day, I'm thinking about the railing—and I know he is, too.

"I wonder if we can get it to come out to the shed," he says one night while we're lying in bed. Honestly, at this point "shed" isn't the right word. It's a cottage, a space we could easily rent out for more than any of the rooms in the inn proper. Best of all, it's tucked away at the back of the property, so we have some privacy. Luca added soundproofing to all of the walls, and he'll add a fence around it soon so we can really be sure that nobody will disturb us.

"Think about it," he continues. "It's fully capable of moving on its own. I bet we could convince it to sneak out to the shed for an hour or two, and it would be back by morning." He trails a finger along my collarbone. "Imagine the fun we could have."

"We can't just leave the inn without a railing! What if someone comes downstairs in the middle of the night and falls? They could be seriously hurt. And we could be seriously sued."

"You're right. What if we add on to the shed and put a staircase in here, and then move the railing here and buy a new one for the inn?" He's joking, but I'm honestly tempted, and he laughs when he catches sight of the look on my face. "Wren, no. *No*," he repeats.

"We're going to the market this weekend. We should look at railings, is all I'm saying. Even if we don't add stairs in here, I'm sure we could find a nice decorative use for it. And then it would be here, with us, ready for all our bedroom needs."

"I do like the sound of that," Luca admits.

So when we get to the market, we shop with that in mind. Luca will probably just end up making something himself, but it's fun looking to see if we can find something.

"Have you been here before?" Luca asks.

I nod. "Yeah, my parents brought me a few times, usually when Brit needed something but didn't have the time to look for it herself. I loved it here. I swore it was magical. Have you been?"

Luca nods. "Never with anyone, though. This is where I come to just be alone."

I look around at the hundreds of people surrounding us. He sees me looking and laughs. "Okay, well, I don't have to talk to them. I don't have responsibilities here, and nobody expects anything from me. I can just get lost in my thoughts while I walk. It's the perfect place to lose yourself: it's huge, has all the same vendors each time, but they're all in different places every time you come. So it's familiar, but not boring, and you'll always find something new. It's the market of dreams."

"Spoken like a poet."

"I am. You know this. In fact, I seem to remember that being part of why you never made a move."

I roll my eyes. "Obviously I was wrong, poets can fuck, too. Happy?"

A woman next to me gasps, scandalized, and I apologize, but I'm laughing so hard there's no way it comes across as sincere.

Luca tugs me into his side and presses a kiss to my temple. "Very."

We wander the market for a few hours, getting lost in the winding paths. Aside from keeping an eye out for railings (which will all be inferior to ours), we don't have a clear goal.

It's nice to have this chance to just be with Luca just the two of us, away from the inn. We hold hands while we walk, and stop for the occasional kiss, and it's nice.

And maybe at the end of it we'll have a plan to get the railing in bed with us.

We're walking down a small side path when Luca stops suddenly and gapes at the tent to our right. It's gorgeous. The tent is made of deep purple fabric and there are scrabble tiles hanging across the front, like strings of beads. "Oh. I recognize the name of this stall. It was on the receipt for the railing."

"Our railing?" What am I saying? Of course he means our railing. "No way. Seriously?"

"Seriously."

"We have to go in." I push through the strings of scrabble tiles across the entrance and give my eyes a second to adjust to the darkness inside. The tent is full closed on three sides, unlike many of the booths at the market, and walking inside almost feels like being transported to another world.

The inside of the tent feels cozy. Homey. But there's something that feels a little magical about it, too.

"Good afternoon." A woman at the back of the tent stands to greet us. She's stunning, maybe around thirty or forty (she has one of those faces that makes it hard to gauge her age), with thick dark hair that falls in waves around her heart-shaped face.

Some shop owners smile at you like they know you're good for a sale.

Some smile at you like they truly love their wares.

Her smile is the latter, full of the kind of quiet passion that can't be faked.

"Hi." I look around, taking in the odd assortment of items. Unlike the other booths at the market, there doesn't seem to be a cohesive theme to the space; there's jewelry; a fine tea set; a beautiful wooden chair; and a million other things that don't make sense together—but also somehow do. "I think my aunt might have bought something here. It would have been a few decades ago. But I'm not sure..."

"What might she have bought?"

"A railing for a staircase?" I don't mean for it to come out as a question, but my voice rises at the end. I expect the woman to tell me I'm wrong, or at least that she doesn't remember a sale from that long ago. She might not have even worked here when Aunt Brit bought it.

But she smiles and nods, and I release the breath I was holding in anticipation.

"I remember it well. A gorgeous piece. And it serves you well?" There's a curious glint in her eye. Is she just a vendor who wants to make sure her customers are satisfied, or does she know exactly how good this railing is at *satisfying* me?

"Very." I can feel myself blushing, so I turn away so she won't notice.

Thankfully, Luca steps in to talk to her while I get myself together. "Her aunt started an inn, which she's running now. With my help," he adds, right as I open my mouth to chastise him for downplaying his own role at the inn yet again. "We recently installed the railing, and it's really made the space come together. I like to think it added a little magic to the place. Wren's been working hard for years, but the moment we installed the railing, things just really seemed to come together. Don't get me wrong, it's her work that's turned things around. But the railing is definitely helping."

There's no way she can hear the innuendo in his words—he's doing a great job of keeping it out of his voice, and the puns are subtly enough even I could have missed them—but it's not helping with the blush burning my face right now.

"My objects are special. Perhaps it truly is providing that little extra something."

"Can I ask...what exactly *is* that little extra something?"

The air seems to go still around us as we all consider Luca's words. Tension thickens between us as we all stare at each other, and two things are clear:

1. None of us are willing to be the one to say it.
2. She absolutely knows.

I really, really hope I'm not somehow wrong about that last bit.

"What if I told you the railing was sentient?" I blurt out, once the silence becomes too much to bear.

"I would ask you to elaborate." There's no surprise in her tone, no shock on her face. She definitely already knew, and now we're locked in this dance of trying not to reveal too much to the other person. Although now that I've broken the ice, it's much easier to keep going.

"I mean that the railing moves on its own. It's polite and cheeky and has a whole personality."

"Polite? Am I to understand the railing speaks?"

I shake my head, partially in answer to her question, and partially at the odd cadence of her speech, like she's a time traveler from a hundred years ago.

"It doesn't speak," I tell her. "But it does a lot of other stuff."

Luca and I tell her about it returning a dropped article of clothing (though we fully gloss over the fact that said article of clothing was a pair of underwear) and how it decorates itself with an attention to detail that's really elevated the inn.

We (obviously) don't tell her about the sex.

"We actually came here today to find a replacement railing for the inn. We didn't know we'd find the vendor Brit sourced it from."

The vendor stiffens at Luca's words, and I swear the temperature in the room drops ten degrees. There's a look in her eye that I can't quite place—anger, but also something deeper and sadder.

Worry, maybe?

Fear?

"You said the railing was to your liking. What do you plan to do with it once you cast it aside?" Her voice is icy, and I take an unconscious step toward Luca.

"Oh, no." Luca turns bright red. "We want to move it to our personal residence. Still on the inn's grounds, and knowing the railing, it will probably still help with the decorations. It's just that we can't seem to find any alone time with the railing."

His eyes widen at the casual implication, even though I'm sure the vendor isn't thinking anything nearly as salacious as the truth. "Which, you know, is a problem because it can't reveal itself to the guests," he stammers. "We thought it would be more comfortable. And we're being a bit selfish, wanting to get some actual time with it."

"There's nothing wrong with the railing," I hurry to confirm. "It *is* to our liking. And it's so beautiful it'll be hard for us to install something else in its place, but we want to move it somewhere it'll have a little more freedom. It deserves to be able to move whenever it wants to."

Just like that, her face smooths over. There's a second where I think I see a glimmer of relief, and then it's gone.

Weird.

I almost ask about her shift in mood, but I catch myself at the last second. She's a stranger, and I'm at her place of business. She doesn't owe me an explanation for why she's feeling whatever it is she's feeling.

Luca and I leave her tent a few minutes later. We plan to walk straight back to the car, but we get distracted multiple times on the way, and it's almost another hour before we make it to the parking lot.

"She was weird, right?" Luca ask as he backs out of the parking spot. "Like, that wasn't just me; her reaction when she thought we were getting rid of the railing was bizarre, right?"

"Definitely."

"What do you think her deal was?"

I honestly don't know.

And for some reason, the farther we drive from the market, the less I care; by the time we reach the inn, I've practically forgotten about the vendor entirely.

CHAPTER NINE

LUCA MAKES a new railing for the inn the next day. It's an exact replica of *our* railing, except it's made of a few pieces instead of just one.

He works astonishingly quickly, and it's finished and fully installed the night before our families are due to arrive. And, because he modeled it perfectly after the current one, it's a breeze to install. We manage to do it while most of the guests are at dinner, and nobody come through during the five minutes it takes to slot the new pieces of wood into place.

When I turn back to the railing we placed on the floor, it's gone.

I spend the night in the shed with him, so I don't have to worry about prepping the rooms once they all get here. He opens the door to greet me with a smile.

Behind him, the railing sits on the wall, resting on pegs that Luca crafted and installed specifically to display the railing.

"You know, we should start calling this place something other than 'the shed.' It's so much more than that now." I look around at the gleaming appliances in the small kitchen, at the bedframe that Luca build himself, and the art he's hung on the walls. The space is absolutely gorgeous. I knew he was good with his hands, but he also has an interior-decorator's eye.

It's so beautiful in here that I never want to leave.

"What should we call it?" He asks. I step inside, and when the door closes behind me, he pulls me in for a deep, lingering kiss. "The cottage? The guest house? *Home?*"

Oh.

I really like the sound of that.

"Yes. Home," I agree.

"*Our* home."

Smooth wood curls around my ankle in a gentle caress, a reminder of the other member of this household.

"How does that sound to you?" I ask the railing.

The length of wood slowly twines around me and Luca, drawing us flush against each other.

Unlike the last time the railing bound us together, this doesn't feel sexual. It feels…loving.

And that's exactly how it fucks us.

Slow and sensual, like we have all the time in the world.

The first press of the wood inside me makes me gasp aloud, and Luca surges forward to capture the sound from my lips.

By the ease with which the wood slides in and out of me, I know it must have reshaped itself a bit—there's no way it would fit so easily in its usual shape. Whatever it's molded itself into is *perfect*. Better than any toy I've had inside me. It stretches me until I'm so full I'm not sure I can take any more, and then it pulls me back onto the bed.

I expect it to fuck me in earnest, but it just holds me still, letting me adjust to the thick, pulsing wood inside me.

And then, the other end trails up Luca's body. He gasps and shudders as the railing twines around his legs, holding them spread apart so he's perfectly on display for me. It teases him slowly, and I watch his erection go from half-mast to so hard it looks like it hurts.

The wood lightly strokes his dick and he jerks in response.

Inside me, the wood presses deeper in perfect sync with Luca's little thrust.

And all the while, Luca's eyes remain on me.

I've watched plenty of people get fucked.

Plenty of people have watched me get fucked.

Hell, I've unknowingly been on both sides of that with Luca for years.

But nothing in my life has ever compared to this experience. The experience of watching Luca get fucked by the very same railing that's fucking me, with in such perfect sync that it almost feels like it's Luca inside me.

Almost, because I can absolutely feel that the thing inside me isn't human.

And when I finally come, hours later, it isn't Luca's name I scream out; it's an incoherent litany of all the things I love about this railing.

The next morning, I look over at the railing as I pick out my clothes for the day. It's twisted itself into a heart, and I reach out to trace a finger along it. It shifts, like it's shivering under my touch, and I lean forward to press a quick kiss to the curve,

"We have time," Luca says from behind me. "You haven't even showered yet."

"I showered last night."

"Yes, but you're about to get so very dirty." He picks me up and tosses me—literally *tosses* me—onto the bed, then crawls onto in, caging me in. He leaves me just enough space to flip over and face him, and only then do I notice he's fully naked.

I take a second to drink him in. He's fucking gorgeous, and I can't believe I spent so many years convincing myself that I couldn't have him, all because of wrong assumptions I made.

"What do you say, Wren?"

"Please?"

He laughs, the super indulgent, low, rich sound that immediately makes me wet. "I was looking more for a yes, but I do love to hear you say please."

"Don't get used to it," I smirk. I like to make him work for it. And, just as often, I like to make *him* beg.

"Oh, there's a lot I could get used to," he says, bending

forward to press a kiss to my collarbone. "But for now, I'm going to show you exactly who's in control."

I bite my lip, trying to decide if I want to fight him for dominance or let him call the shots today. But before I can make up my mind, the weight of his body suddenly rolls off me. Cool air rushes into the space he was filling, and I pout as I look over at him.

He's trapped, fully bound by thin bands of wood at his ankles, hips, and chest.

"Guess you're not the one in charge today," I smirk. I'll have to find a way to reward the railing for taking my side in this sexy little power struggle.

But a second later, I'm pinned to the bed, too. "Oh," I gasp. "I guess I'm not the one in control, either." I wriggle, testing the strength of the railing, and it tightens. The more I try to move, the less I'm able to.

The railing has left my hands free, so I reach down to pull my underwear off. I've barely touched the fabric when the railing catches my wrist and pulls it away, gently pressing it against the mattress. Then, with deliciously maddening slowness, it drags my panties down my legs.

And then it…

Does nothing.

After all the teasing last night, I expected today to be more like the first time, hard and fast and desperate. But it turns out, our railing likes to toy with us. I love it, but I'm also desperate to get off.

"God, Wren, you look…" Luca breaks off with a thick swallow. His eyes rove my body, finally landing between my thighs. "Say please and I might take care of that for you. If I'm allowed."

I turn my head and glare at him as severely as I can manage through my haze of lust. "You already got one 'please' out of me today; don't be greedy."

"Fine, then I guess I'll just have to use my hand on myself." He smirks, and my eyes drop down to watch his hand stroke his dick. One, two, three pumps, and then the railing pulls his hand away, too.

"I need—"

But I don't have a chance to finish the sentence before I feel something brush against my clit. I gasp, and instinctively try to jerk my hips, but they're held firmly in place. So I feel every brush of the wood against my slick core. I don't know why I'm so sensitive but it's almost more than I can bear, and I'm suddenly very glad for the soundproofing Luca added to the shed, because the noises coming out of me are decidedly not guest friendly.

"Oh, fuck," Luca breathes beside me. I look down to see that the railing has wrapped around his dick and is contracting around him in slow pulses. He moans, a high-pitched, desperate sound that is utterly depraved.

When he moans a second time, the railing slides inside me.

The feeling coupled with the sound Luca makes leaves me weak, and I gasp.

I turn my head and find Luca's eyes on me. They're wild and hungry, and I learn forward as much as I can, drawing him into a sloppy kiss. Luca drags his tongue along my bottom lip and nips it gently. I moan, and he bites harder. The little jolt of pain sends a bolt of pleasure shooting through me, and I moan against his mouth.

The railing chooses that exact moment to push further inside me. It starts up a slow, steady rhythm, completely at odds with the sharp pinpricks of pain Luca leaves on my lips, and the disparate sensations drive me fucking wild.

Luca jerks beside me then breaks the kiss with a deep, guttural moan. My gaze drops from his lips, down his chest, and further down to his dick, which the railing is working at the same tempo as it's thrusting into me. A bead of precum glistens on the tip of his dick and I ache at the sight of it. I want to bend forward and take him in my mouth, lick that little burst of flavor from his tip, then take him deeper in my mouth.

But I'm bound.

And the fact that I can't do what I want has me just as turned on. Looking at Luca, I can see that the same is true for him: he wants me, and he loves that he can't have me.

But then the pressure on my wrist eases, and the moment I'm able, I reach out to grab his perfect length in my hand. My movements are clumsy, half-bound as I am, as my hand and the railing fight to be the one to stroke Luca's dick.

"Fuck," Luca whispers. "Fu—" But he's cut off mid-word as the railing covers his mouth.

Luca's eyes go wide, and then he's shuddering, his cried muffled by the wood against his lips. His dick pulses in my hand, covering my fingers in his cum.

The railing speeds up inside me, fucking me hard and fast, and it doesn't take long for me to follow Luca over the edge.

The railing slides out of me, and I clench around it, desperate to keep it inside me even though I've just been so thoroughly fucked I can barely move.

"Wren," Luca groans.

"I know."

"Fuck."

I grin. "Again, I know."

The railing trails along my skin, and I grab it, feeling the slick evidence of Luca's orgasm on the polished wood.

"Luca," I pout. "You made a mess. Clean it up."

Without taking his eyes off me, Luca leans forward and licks the railing clean. He takes his time, making sure he gets every last drop as the railing shivers against his tongue.

"Was that what you had in mind when you suggested a little diversion?" I ask as I stand and grab the clothes I intended to put on before…well, all of that.

"I don't think I called it a diversion."

"Whatever." I laugh. "I think it's safe to say you've made me very, very late."

"You don't mind. Because you're not actually on the schedule today."

"Okay, yes, but I should go over and check on things."

"And you will." He pulls me up his body and presses a sweet kiss to my lips. "After you've showered. Because I was right: you definitely need one now."

Luca is right, of course.

After I take the faster shower of my life, which I refuse to let him join me for, and get dressed (for real this time) I head over to the main building…and there's nothing for me to do.

The new staff is running things smoothly, all the guests are happy, and I can truly just enjoy my day off. Which is so out of the ordinary that I find things to do anyway. I apologize to the staff, but they get it. This place is my labor of love, and after coming so close to losing it, I'm just not willing to take any risks. Besides, they know me well enough by now to know that it's my own neurosis making me triple check their work, and not any distrust in them.

Thankfully, they all seem to understand. But I think they're all relived when my family arrives and pulls my attention off of them.

Aunt Brit sweeps through the front door like the owns the place, which is fair, considering she literally did own it—for longer than I've been alive.

"Oh, Wren," she says, pressing a hand to her heart. "The place looks good. It's…wow."

"You like it?"

"It's somehow exactly the same and so very different. Still the inn I built, but I can see even just from here that you've made it your own. It's perfect." She sweeps me into a hug, and it's only when I melt into her that I realize just how tense I've been, waiting for her approval—and not entirely sure I'd get it.

"I'm glad you think so."

"She's not the only one. Move, Brit, let me get to my daughter." My mom hip-checks her sister aside and pulls me into a hug that smells like cinnamon and nutmeg, which are, somehow, her year-round scents. She's not even a baker. And yet, it works for her. "You'll have to give us the grand tour later, but first I want to catch up. Tell me what's new in your life."

"Bethany," my dad chides from behind her. "Let *me* get a chance to say hello to my daughter, too."

My mom laughs an apology and steps aside so my dad can hug me.

"Hey, birdie. Missed you."

"I missed you too, dad."

Gracie brings out a tray of food and the four of us sit on the back patio. I tell them about the renovations and about the little bit of gardening I've been doing. I share some stories about guests, mindful of the fact that any of the current ones could come outside and overhear us.

"That all sounds so lovely," my mother says, wiping away a tear. "You seem like you're doing very well."

"I am," I confirm.

"And what about your love life? Any men on the horizon?" She sounds as hopeful as she always does, and for once I don't have to disappoint her.

"Well…"

My mother screeches. Like, actually honest to god *screeches*.

Luca comes running to make sure everything is okay, and she looks up at him, embarrassed.

"Sorry Luca, Wren here just told us that she's seeing someone."

"She hasn't technically told us anything yet," Brit says with a little frown. "She implied it. You did imply it, right? You're seeing someone?" She turns to me with a little glare that pins me in place.

"Yes."

"Who is it?" My mother demands. And then, when I don't answer in literally one second, she keeps going. "Is he local? Do we know him? Luca, do you know who this mystery man is?"

"I do." He blushes, and my mom's mouth drops open.

"Not *you*? Oh, please tell me it's you. Wren, I'm going to be very disappointed if it isn't Luca, now you've gone and gotten all my hopes up."

"I haven't done anything," I protest weakly.

Her face falls. "Oh."

"But yes, it is Luca."

This time, my mother lets out a noise that I can only imagine is a perfect impersonation of a banshee.

"That's about how I felt when I found out," a voice says behind me, and now it's my turn to scream.

"Lucy!" I launch myself at my best friend, and she stumbles back, barely managing to stay upright.

"I'm so glad I didn't miss the Wren and Luca Dating story. I've gotten bits and pieces of it, of course, but I need to know everything. Tell us."

She pulls up a chair, and I drop back into mine.

The six of us stay on the patio until dinner is served, and then Luca and I give everyone the tour. I watch Brit the whole time, bracing for disappointment, but there is none. She looks content, and…proud.

"You've done good. Really good."

I'm still glowing when I fall into bed with Luca that night and fall asleep to the sound of a storm picking up outside. And I'm still glowing when I hear a loud crash in the middle of the night.

But I'm not glowing when I run outside and inventory the damage that a fallen limb has done to the inn.

There are branches everywhere, and random debris scattered around the grounds. The cleanup won't be fun, but with my family here, it should be pretty easy to deal with.

What'll be less easy to deal with?

The hole in the goddamn roof.

CHAPTER TEN

I CALL the insurance adjuster the moment their office opens. Thankfully none of the guests are hurt, and there's only damage to one of the rooms (you know, the room with the *giant fucking hole in the roof*), but after everything we've been through over the past few years, but setback feels insurmountable.

Luca rubs my back the whole time I talk to the insurance agent, and when my tears choke me, Aunt Brit silently takes the phone. It's the same agent she used to work with, and they had a close enough relationship that things go much more quickly once she takes over. Thank god she was here; I don't know how I would have handled it without her.

It's silly; I've handled everything else. But this just feels like the cherry on the sundae. The straw that breaks the camel's back.

And it happened just before her birthday, too, so she can't even enjoy it like she wanted to.

"Nonsense." She waves a hand. "I'll bunk with your parents, Lucy will take my room, the guests in that room will enjoy a discounted stay in the room Lucy's booked for, and everything will work out okay.

"You're not bunking with my parents. Not on your birthday."

So that's how I end up recreating the sleepovers from my childhood: the guests move into Lucy's room, and she stays in the shed-slash-cottage-slash-*home*. I thought the days of me, Lucy, and Luca all piled into one giant bed were long over, but despite the awful reason for it, I'm giddy at the beginning of our sleepover.

"Absolutely no sex," Lucy demands as we all pile onto the bed.

"Oh my god, Luce, obviously." I roll my eyes at her.

"Think about how little you want to witness your twin having sex," Luca says in disgust. "Now think about how much worse it would be for your twin to witness *you* having sex. You think I could perform with you in the same room? Let alone in the same bed?" Luca gags, and I can't tell if it's dramatic effect or if it's real. I wouldn't blame him either way.

"That's a good point." Lucy sniffs. "Okay, in as few detail as possible, please tell me everything you left out in the version your parents got."

We do, skipping over the sex that first night. We tell her that we've both had feelings for ages, but that we both thought it was unrequited—and that neither of us thought she meant it when she said we should be together.

"I mean, yeah, the idea of it was kind of weird," she says. "Luca's my brother and I see Wren as a sister, so it's like my siblings are dating. But *you two* aren't siblings, so…" She shrugs.

"Thank god for that," Luca and I say at the same time.

Lucy narrows her eyes at us and we all three break into laughter.

Luca and I lock eyes, having a silent conversation about just how much to withhold from her. I nod, and he sighs.

"Okay. This next thing. We won't give any details, but we do have to acknowledge the sex in order to tell you about it."

"Is it weird kinky shit?" she asks, her eyes darting to me.

"I mean… it's not *not* weird kinky shit?" I shrug. That's the best I can truthfully give her.

"Ugh. Do I really need to know?"

"Trust me, you'd be madder if we didn't tell you."

Haltingly, we tell her about the railing. She clearly thinks we're making it up—until Luca nods at the wood over our bed, which is moving on its own, twisting along the wall until it's spelled out a cursive word: hi.

"Holy fucking shit." Lucy scrambles backward, her eyes wide. "That's... you're not messing with me. That's really happening."

"Yep."

"Who knows?"

"Just us," I tell her.

"Not Gracie?"

"Not really keen on telling my employee she's working in a haunted inn."

"She's not just your employee, though; she's your friend," Lucy pushes just enough to make me remember the crush she used to have on Gracie in high school. Not that it matters; Lucy isn't going to stop traveling the world any time soon, and Gracie has never had any interest in leaving our town. But still, maybe while Lucy is in town I can gently nudge the two of them together.

"Yeah, she's also my friend. My friend who would run for the hills if she knew about this."

"Maybe not. I think she'd take it better than you think," Lucy says.

"Maybe. I'll think about it."

Lucy is still staring at the railing. It slithers off the wall and she scrambles backward. "Nope. Uh-uh. I don't swing that way."

"I didn't think I did, either," Luca says. "Don't knock it 'til you try it."

"Ew. Stop. That's enough sex talk from you."

We put on a movie soon after that, and the three of us fall asleep in a pile of limbs, just like we did when we were kids.

The contractor comes out the next morning, and he makes a beeline for Aunt Brit when he arrives, but she sends him my way. "My niece is the proprietor now," she says with so much pride in her voice I swear she's going to burst.

"Oh, I'm well aware," the contractor says under his breath. Thankfully, Brit doesn't seem to hear him. He explains to me the work that needs to be done. Thankfully, the tree didn't break anything load-bearing. We'll need to replace part of the wall and the roof, and it'll be hard to find a window to match the old, original glass in the place, but the tree didn't cause any major structural damage.

It's the first time something has gone wrong that didn't feel like it could possibly bring about the end of the inn. We're only down one room, and the repairs should be done in under a week.

By the time my parents, Brit, and Lucy leave, the inn is almost back to its usual condition, and my confidence has skyrocketed. This is the first emergency we've faced since business picked up, and we came out the other side mostly unscathed.

"Maybe it really is the railing, that turned things around" I say the night our family leaves. I'm lying in bed with Luca, in what we are now officially referring to as our home. The first thing I did after my family left was move the rest of my things into the shed. "If that tree had fallen six months ago, it would have taken out the whole back of the inn."

It could have, too. The thing was *huge*, and apparently old enough that it needed to come down soon, anyway. I've called a local arborist, who'll be out soon to do a full survey of all of the trees on the property.

In the meantime, I have an inn full of guests, employees I like and trust, and the approval of the woman who opened this inn with nothing but a dream and a few bucks in her pocket a few decades ago.

"You're definitely at least a *little* responsible," Luca says, trailing kisses down my stomach.

Above us, the railing twists itself into a single word: you.

I shake my head. "I'll take some of the credit, but definitely not all of it."

"Hmm." Luca rolls over until he's on top of me, then bends forward until his lips are barely brushing my own. "I think we might need to force you to accept your role in restoring this place to its former glory."

And that is exactly what he and the railing do.

ACKNOWLEDGMENTS

Thank you, as always, to Bailey, for the blurbs. I don't know what I would have done without you.

And, of course, thanks to bi+ book gang and the cottage. Thanks for holding my hand and cheering me on and coming along for the ride. I will always and forever appreciate y'all.

When I picked up the first sentient object book I ever read, I went into it expecting silly fun—and it absolutely delivered on that front, but I wasn't expecting the amount of heart in it. I'm not claiming that my own books are super groundbreaking or anything, but many of the books I've read in this genre blend the funny and absurd with some really powerful emotional journeys, social commentary, and other elements that make them really resonate with a lot of people.

So for this series, that's what you can expect. Silly smut with a hefty dose of a character journey for the MC. Don't get me wrong, you can probably expect some stories from me in the future that are purely silly bullshit fun, because those stories absolutely have a place, and I've personally clung to those types of stories as a lifeline.

In the meantime, if this is your first sentient object romance (and even if it's not), I recommend looking into some of the other authors writing in this genre. Whether you're looking for silly fun, titillation, emotional journeys, or social commentary (or some blend of those), I can pretty much guarantee there's someone writing what you're looking for.

ALSO BY ANNARA LAYNE

Sentient Object Romance
Objects of Desire

Bedding the Bedding

Plowing the Plow

Railing the Railing

* * *

Other Works
Obscure Holidays Erotica Collection (short stories)

Polar Bear Plunge

Clean off your Desk Day

Ditch New Year's Resolution Day

Hot Sauce Day

Eat Ice Cream for Breakfast Day

Work Naked Day

International Condom Day

Random Act of Kindness Day

Tell a Fairy Tale Day

Dentists Day

Napping Day

Awkward Moments Day

Make Up Your Own Holiday Day

Obscure Holidays Short Story Collection: Volume I